Nightmare:

"Jake please don't!! I don't know what I did please!!" I pleaded as I clung to his shirt and tears poured down my face.

He has always protected me I don't understand what is going on.

He looks down at me and for a second I see a softness in his eyes but it is quickly replaced with a hard glare.

"Don't fucking touch me!" He spat as he grabs my hands and throws me to the ground before leaving locking the door behind him, leaving me alone in the dark with nothing but my silent sobs.

"Please Jake don't leave me in the dark!" I cried out as I ran up to the door and started pounding on it but it was usless.

I turned to walk away from the door but I didn't get far when the door flung open, I spun around just in time to be picked up by my throat and slammed against the wall so hard I lost my breath.

struggling to breathe I gasp and look up and immediately start shaking. This man was massive and stunk of alcohol, he looked at me with so much rage I was instantly terrified

"please Stop." I cried terrified and just wanting to be home

"Stop your whining its disgusting." he snarled throwing me to the ground causeing me to hit my head rather hard

"Now get up and fight!" he rawred making me jump. I don't understand why he wanted me to fight im just nine years old, I would never be able to fight him.

"I said Fight!" he yelled as he charged over to me and kicked me hard in my stomach making me scream out in pain
and cry even harder.

"Disgusting. you will learn to fight or you will die." he said as he walked to the door and left me bleeding on the ground.

I felt the blood trickle down my head as everything started spinning and slowly went black. Im alone...

Chapter One: Lay Low

JAYS P.O.V.

I jerked up from my bed breathing rapidly and covered in a cold sweat. It was the same old nightmare as every night only it isn't just a bad dream,
its the first memory I have of my life being taken away at such a young age. I took a deep breath and looked over at my clock it was four in the morning, I haven't slept more then four or five hours a night since I got here. I guess its the constant fear of them finding me again I mean it is the third
time I have had to move states in the past year and a half. I brushed the thoughts aside and got out of bed if I don't get my mind off of them then
im gonna have another attack and I cant deal with that right now.

I walked down the hall and to my home gym and flipped on the lights. it wasn't to big just a few punching bags and a treadmill. I wrapped my knuckles and proceeded to do what I do best...Train.

My name is Jay Moore, I am seventeen years old. When I was eight I lost my father, then at age nine my Mom passed. At age nine I lost my

freedom as well, after many beatings and tortures I finally gave into my captors and agreed to try and fight. They trained me till age twelve and put me in my first underground street fight and I won, that was the first night in a while Mason didn't come into my cell and beat me... I even got a warm meal.
I remained undefeated but the beatings kept coming and at age fourteen I snapped... needless to say I was able to escape and have been running every since. Every time I believe I can truly settle down somewhere they find me. I can't trust anyone and I definetly can not draw any attention to myself. I got to California a month ago and start school in a few hours. I live on my own on the edge of town. Though underground street fighting is extremely dangerous and was something I was forced into it kind of became a clutch for me. the only way I can deal with any of my pain and anxiety is with gloves now. fighting became apart of me and something I cant mentally live without, something nobody can ever take away from me. Though I am trying to keep my head down I need the fights so I fight under a secret identity named demon, and trust me When I Say Demon is known but Jay isn't and im planning to keep it that way.

I glance at the clock and its already five-thirty so I decide that's enough for now and go to take a shower and get ready for school.
its not that I really need to go to school because I make plenty of money from my fights its more that im just trying to fit in. it is a small town on the edge of Cali so if I go into town for supplies then its best to be a regular kid in school rather then the mysterious town talk about. I lock up and walk towards an amazing perk of the fight night money, my 67 Chevy impala I mean come on this car is a beast! I can't help but smile as she rawrs to life, I head to school trying to put my nerves aside. I am fine, they will not find me this time. I tried to

reassure myself as I pulled up to the school. there were a few kids outside but luckily not many, I parked my baby and walked towards the school smirking at the gawking eyes studying my car... I know she's sexy.

I kept my head down and made my way towards my locker, luckily I got the full tour a few days prior so I knew where to go. Remember don't draw attention, don't draw attention, don't draw...and just like that I felt myself run slap into someone and as gravity pulled me downward before I felt an arm snake around my waist sending sparks up my spine and spin me around holding me up making me meet an icy pair of blue eyes and I lost my breath. He had jet black hair mostly covered by a red baseball cap and was a foot or so taller then me. I could find myself able to easily get lost in his eyes and I quickly snapped back to reality clearing my throat as I stood up straight taking a step back.

"you should keep your head up angel." he said with a cocky smirk. Ugh i don't have time for this idiot...stupid jocks

"Jay" was all I said giving him a blank look before turning to walk away but i pause and glance back at him
" and if you knew me, you would never call me angel again." I said with a smirk and walked to my locker.

"Hey you must be Jay! I'm Meg very nice to meet you." I turned to see a short brunet with brown eyes smiling at me, she was pretty and seemed sweet so i gave her a small smile.

"Nice to meet you too." i said back to her and she looked as if she were going to say something but looked over my shoulder and immediately went

silent and eyes wide. i looked to see a tall skinny blonde with a bit to much make-up coming my way with a look on her face i know all to well, hate.
i turned back to my locker and sighed, 'what now' i thought and turned around to face the drama heading my way.

"Um and who do you think you are?" she spat with a nasty glare clearly trying to intimidate me... yeah not gonna happen.

"I saw that little stunt with Caiden earlier and I am here to make it clear that he is MINE! so back off bitch!" she said taking a challenging step towards me but i kept a look of boredom as i slid my bag off my shoulder and sitting it on the ground before taking a step towards her.

"Let me guess your the schools queen Bee right... treats everyone else like crap. well let me make one thing clear i don't give a Fuck who you are you will show me some respect or you will leave me the hell alone." i couldn't help but let out a devilish smirk as i leaned forward just a little "i would hate for you to get hurt" i said and turned grabbing my bag before giving her one last glance and i noticed the boy from earlier that i now know is Caiden watching us and i looked back at her.

"I'm jay and im in no way interested in your little boy toy so back off." and with that i walked away leaving everyone staring at little miss Barbie wide eyed and trying not to laugh.

so much for laying low.

"Hey wait up!" i turned to see meg catching up to me with a huge grin on her face

"Your officially my new best friend! Meet me at lunch ill introduce you to my other bestie Danny?" she asked as the bell rang and i nodded before heading to gym class.

we were running laps today which worked for me because running was part of my daily training anyhow,
plus i needed to blow off a little steam because i have already drawn to much attention to myself.
i had my headphones in as i was running laps when i felt someone tap on my shoulder.
pulling out my headphones i turned to look at a tall blonde with hazel eyes and brod shoulders smiling at me.

"Uh hey i saw you talking to Meg briefly before the bell rang after your badass stand off and figured i would go ahead and introduce myself I'm Danny."
he said holding out his hand making me smile in realization remembering meg mention him.

"Right Meg mentioned you, I'm Jay." i say shaking his hand and we continue to walk so we wouldn't get yelled at by the coach.

"Sounds about right. That was impressive this morning, people don't really stand up to Beth like that." he said still holding that smile.

"So that's her name. What's her major malfunction anyhow?" i asked putting a name to Barbie

"Ah usually she's easy to ignore unless it has to do with Caiden. She's crazy when it comes to him,
i almost feel bad for the dude because they aren't even dating but if you steer clear of him then she shouldn't be a problem."
he stated as we continued to walk. Definitely shouldn't be an issue then. We walked and talked for the remainder
of gym and turns out we are a lot alike. of course he got the edited version of my life but he reminds me of my older brother before he changed.
even made the comment of me reminding him of his sister that lives with his father, i can tell he misses her.

"I'll see you at lunch jay" he said with a smile before walking away to get ready for second period.

i changed and headed to second period and it was still empty when i got there.
i walked to the very back and sat down glancing at the clock i still had five minutes before class starts so i got out my book and began reading. i was so lost in my story that i didn't notice anyone entered the room till i heard the seat pull out right next to me. i glance over to be met with those same icy blue eyes that has already caused to much attention for me,
what could he possibly want now?

"Hey there Angel." He said with that stupid smirk plastered on his face.
i gave him a blank look before rolling my eyes and turning back to my book.
he was still staring at me so i huffed and closed my book before turning to glare at him.

"What." i said through gritted teeth getting very annoyed with his attention.

" That was an impressive show you put on earlier." He said smiling at me ignoring my bad mood
Before i got a chance to respond or bust him upside the head, my phone started ringing and
there's only one person with my number, i look down and as i thought it was Xavier my boss of the underground fights
and the only person on earth i trust. When i escaped a few years ago he took me in and finished my training.
Every time they found me he got me out just in time. He was like my father but he was also a real pain in the ass and i knew not to ignore his call.

"What's up X." i say sounding bored as usual

"Demon we got a problem with tonight's fight! you need to meet me now! move your ass.
I'm at east point garage roof top." he said sounding rigid, this cant be good.

"Be there in fifteen, ten if traffics good." was all i said before hanging up and grabbing my stuff walking out before the teacher got there and ignoring the confused expression on Caiden's face.

Lay Low Jay.

JAY'S P.O.V.

JAY'S P.O.V:

Pulling into East Point Garage I noticed the place was pretty empty as i circled each level making my way to the Rooftop Parking.
When I got out there i saw Xaiver pacing next to his truck. i parked across from him and got out of the car, as i made my way to him
i took notice of his messy blonde hair which is usually well kept. Looks like he has been pulling at his hair stressing like crazy
which worried me because as long as i have known X he is always calm and well preserved but right now he looks unhinged. X was tall and in his late thirty's early forty's age range, never really asked.
i walked up to him and watched as he paced and paced and paced not saying a word to me.

"Whats up X?" i asked as i observed the stress in his eyes. he stopped pacing and faced me but still not speaking to me just studying me intently.
this is starting to get aggravating, i rolled my eyes and shifted my weight staring at him just as hard. "You gonna tell me why im here or do i have to guess?"
i asked trying not to sound tense.

"I finished up my meeting this morning and came back to my office to find Raider sitting there." he paused taking a deep breath giving that a second to sink in.
My heart dropped at his name but i didn't let myself react i just waited for him to continue.

"He said he is going to get you back one way or another no matter the consequences and said to let you know he will see you soon.
Jay if he knows about your fight tonight he is likely to show up. i think you should lay low for a little while, dodge outta a couple fights till he thinks you left again." at this point his words were a mile a minute and i could tell he was really worried.

"Hey X, calm down. Breathe, I'm good honest. I can handle Raider and there is no way in hell I'm gonna miss this or any other fight.
You and I both know that one day I am going to have to face my past, might as well face some of it here, now. Plus you will be there... I'm good."

I gave him a reassuring smile and looked him in the eyes not letting any of my fear show and he started relaxing.
He took a deep breath and nodded his head knowing im not gonna back outta a fight.

"I'll be here by seven to train for tonight's fight." i said giving him a nod

"Please be careful Demon." he said and eyes holding the up most sincerest urgency, i gave him a simple nod and turned to go back to my car.
Looking at my phone third period was halfway over meaning id get back just in time for lunch. As I drove back to school i couldn't help but to let my thoughts surround Xaiver's words.
Raider... God it had been two years since i seen that asshole. Raider and i use to fight together, we also dated for almost a year. We were an unstoppable tag team and extremely close but i didn't take to kindly to finding him in the closet with a fightnight groupie.
I have not seen him since that night but what scares me most is how close we got. Raider knows a lot about my past and i can't help but fear how far he is willing to go to get me back.

By the time i got back to the school my mind was racing as well as my heart. Trying to shake the thoughts out of my head i took a deep breath and headed inside and towards the lunchroom. The halls weren't to crowded but enough for me to know lunch had started recently. I walked into the lunchroom and spotted Meg and Danny at the back table and i made my way straight to them, i was definitely to stressed to eat right now anyhow.

"Hey! Where were you?" Meg asked as i sat next to her.

"Yeah we thought you had Physics with us but didn't see you." Danny piped in

"Awe you guy's missing me already" i said batting my eyes as we all laughed

"Yea yea yea" Danny smiled nudging meg with his elbow making her grin

I was about to ask if something was going on between them but didn't get the chance as water poured over my face and chest making
me jump up to my feet and spin around "WHAT THE FUCK!" i yelled making the lunchroom go silent as my eye lock on Beths face.

"Now that i have your attention i will say this one last time... Back off Caiden he is so not gonna end up with you!" Beth spat at me
but i didn't even process what she was saying. I don't know if it was the ice cold water or the lack of sleep or even the news about raider
but something in me snapped and everything went red, before i knew what was going on i had delivered a descent right hook to beth making her fall on the floor clutching her jaw crying out and one of the girls with her tried to swing on me but i quickly dodged it giving her a gut
punch followed by swiftly jerking my knee up catching her nose as she fall to the ground. i look around and see people staring at us wide

eyed and others trying not to laugh, i look over at meg and danny and they had grins a mile wide. i couldn't be here right now... i had to get outta here. I grabbed my bag and took off to my car... i needed to get to the gym and train...i needed to slow my mind down, i cant deal with this right now. I got into my car and took off towards the gym. So much for laying low, stupid! I didn't even know Caiden...we haven't even had a actual conversation! ugh this is bullshit!

I pulled into the gym and didn't bother slowing down as i went through the doors past X and one of the newest trainees. They both look at me but don't say anything to me as i make my way to the punching bags and started wrapping my knuckles. I heard Xaiver mumble something about giving me some time to the guy next to him before turning back to their conversation. I walked up to the punching bag and gave it everything i had, each hit after the other harder then the last. I feel myself being pulled outta my mental zone by an extreme exhaustion, i am not sure how long i have been at it but my body was clearly telling me its time to take a break. i clung to the bag taking rapid breaths trying to maintain my balance before going to sit down on the bench. Not a second passed before Xaiver was sitting next to me with a bottle of water waiting for me to talk. I grabbed the bottle and took a few long gulps before taking a deep breath then turning to look at him, i frowned looking into his eye because i hate seeing him so worried all because of me. i proceeded to tell him about all about my first day and though he was tense through most the story, he lightened up when i mentioned kicking their asses he even laughed which made me smile.

"Come on let's train." i said as i got up to the treadmill to begin my training.

I have to focus on This fight, my competitor is their local Champion by the name of Brute the Brutal.

Now given this is a small town they don't have a lot to offer in favor of decent fighters but I will give him due credit, he has held his title as champion for the last three years but when watching his videos i noticed he throws a lot of his weight into his punches which can be very effective for a quick win but also can come at a disadvantage for him if i play this right, all there is left to do is find his weak point and its game over.

cAIDEN'S P.O.V.

CAIDEN'S P.O.V.

I woke up to my alarm going off ruining a very peaceful sleep. God i do not wanna go to this place i thought as i grabbed my phone silencing it. I quickly got ready and headed downstairs to find my little sister May watching cartoon's and my mom cooking breakfast, i couldn't help but smile. Those two are my whole world and now that my father has passed on it is my responsibility to take care of them.

"Hey sweetie, you hungry?" My mom asked me when she noticed me in the doorway.

"No im alright i gotta get an early start to avoid hallway traffic." i smiled at her

"CAAAIIDDEENN!!" May yelled running up to me arms stretched wide. i picked her up giving her a big hug.

"Hey babygirl, i got to get going but ill take you to the arcade Saturday sound good?" i asked earning me a huge smile and lots of nods as i sat her down and she ran back to her show.

"Later mom love you." i said walking out the door

"Love you too" she yelled. I closed the door and walked out to my Pride and Joy. I know its very stereotypical for me to be all about my car but its a 65 GTO with sweet candy red body work, I smile as i take her in. The car use to be my fathers but when he passed away my mother gave it to me as a project car and i just finished it up over the summer, i think i did pretty good if i do say so myself. I pulled up to the school and took notice that there aren't many cars here yet so maybe I'm early enough. I parked my car and headed to my locker, in all honesty i wasn't to concerned about hallway traffic as much as i was about running into Beth. The girl is mental!! I do not do the boyfriend thing because i don't have time for it and she knew this when we hooked up...ONE TIME. but that's all it took and the chick is an addict, scaring off any woman who looks my way. i peered around the corner and let out a breath i didn't know i was holding in, she wasn't here yet.
I quickly opened my locker and turned to leave not wanting to be here when she got here, but was definitely thrown off by someone not paying attention and running straight into me. Out of instinct in instantly reached out and wrapped my arm around their waist swinging them around and pulling them into me. All the aggravation and irritation i felt toward this person vanashed when our eyes locked.
She had deep Bright green eyes with gold flecks swimming all through them like fire dancing, she had long jet black hair that fell just above her waist.

I don't know how long we were staring at each other before she cleared her throat and took a couple steps back making me miss the warmth of having her that close to me.

"you should keep your head up angel." I said giving a little smirk.

"Jay" was all she said giving me a blank look that had me stumped...most girls love my attention. She turned to walk away but stoped giving me a sideways glance " and if you knew me, you would never call me angel again." she said with a smirk and walked to what i think is her locker. She acted as though she could care less which was new for me. i couldn't help but watch her as she talked to Meg over by what im assuming is her locker.

I was watching her intently give meg what looks like an honest to God smile but it doesn't Quite reach her eyes.
Suddenly i could feel my body tense up when i notice beth staring at me across the hall while im staring at jay, the thing that made me tense up was beth walking straight to Jay getting ready to do what she does best... be a bitch.
Anytime i give any chick an ounce of attention Beth goes nuts and scares them all off, not that i care cause they are all the same around here but im not even dating her and shes still being possessive. I watched as Jay turned to face her with a bored expression on her face.

"Um and who do you think you are?" Beth spat with a nasty glare clearly trying to scare her as usual but looking at Jay it doesn't look like that's gonna happen.

"I saw that little stunt with Caiden earlier and I am here to make it clear that he is MINE! so back off bitch!" Beth yelled as she sickingly claimed me and taking a challenging step towards her but the look of boredom never left Jays face as she slid her bag off her shoulder and sat it on the ground before taking a step towards Beth showing no fear and absolute control..

"Let me guess your the schools queen Bee right... treats everyone else like crap. well let me make one thing clear i don't give a Fuck who you are you will show me some respect or you will leave me the hell alone." I could have sworn Jay let out a smirk when she said this as if she were enjoying all this. "i would hate for you to get hurt" Jay said and she turned and grabbed her bag before giving beth one last glance.

"I'm jay and im in no way interested in your little boy toy so back off." and with that she walked away leaving everyone wanting to know more about her whether that was her intent or not. Who was this girl?

Throughout the first period my mind was very full of questions about her. Where did she come from? Why does it seem like she was carrying so much behind those eyes? Does she really not feel any attraction towards me? so on and so forth, i met up with the only two people outside my family i have ever given a crap about, Mike and Tyler. They are brothers, Fraternal twins to be exact, Mike is tall with black hair and is definitely known as the jock out of the two while Tyler on the other hand is a half a foot shorter with Blonde hair and he was always extremely quiet. i have known them since i was seven we actually met because someone was picking on Ty and i jumped in to make them go on somewhere, a few minutes later Mike came running from inside to check on Ty... we have been best friends since then, brothers.

As we were walking laps in gym i was pulled from my train of thought when i overheard what Mike and Ty were talking about.

"Dude that showdown this morning was badass!" Mike said referring to Beth and Jays Conversation in the halls.

"Yea wasn't that about you?" Ty added on looking at me smirking, how he finds Beth's constant torture over me funny i don't even know.

"Just Beth's usual bullshit." i said through gritted teethe.

"Beth yes but that new chick? Nobody ever shows that much grit towards people like beth, kinda sexy if you ask me."
Mike said with a shrug and i instantly tensed not liking where this was going. "I mean I wouldn't mind getting to know
her a little bit if you know what i mean." He continued as he winked at us and it made me clench my jaw, not gonna happen.

"Her name is Jay, stop trying to get in her pants you haven't even met her dude." i said trying not to make it obvious i
didn't like what he had to say about her. They both just looked at each other and started smirking before continuing the laps.
Stupid twin crap i swear they can read each others minds sometimes, I don't like it.

"Hey you guy's hear about the fight tonight? Apparently the head guys set Brute up with a big fight tonight you guys wanna go?"
Mike asked changing the subject. Every so often we would go to watch the underground fights to get our mind off of things, it was
definitely something to distract you. Our local Champion has held his title for Three years now, i guess that's why he is Brute the Brutal.

"Yea im down" i said needing a distraction from those damn Green eyes running through my mind. Ty simply nodded in agreement.
We didn't talk anymore about Jay throughout first period as we finished up our laps. when the bell rang we each went our separate way and headed for class. Lucky for me my class was right next door so i got there about five minutes early. i was fully planning on sitting at the very front, needing to focus on my studies instead of some new girl but all my plans went down the toilet when i stepped through the door. In the very back was the girl i was hoping to stop thinking about, she hadn't noticed me walk into the room because she was burried in some book. before i knew what i was doing i was already in the back of the room sitting down right next to her. She looked up from her book finally but when she saw it was me i could have swore she looked annoyed seeing me.

"Hey there Angel." I said giving her a slight smile. She gave me a blank look before rolling her eyes and turning back to her book.
What the hell...nothing, not even a smile. She huffed and closed her book before turning to glare at me.

"What." She said through gritted teeth though her annoyance didn't reach her eyes.

" That was an impressive show you put on earlier." I said smiling at her ignoring the put on annoyance coming from her.
She was about to say something but was cut short by her phone going off and i couldn't help but look at the phone, it was someone named Xaiver.

"What's up X." She said sounding bored.

she tensed up before replying "Be there in fifteen, ten if traffics good."
with that she grabbed her stuff and turned then left not sparing me even a glance.

"This isn't over Angel." i mumbled to myself.

you can probably guess how second period went, i couldn't focus at all. i mean where was she going this early into school? Plus who could she possibly know here anyhow that she would jump up for? Boyfriend maybe, that would explain why she won't give me the time of day, Loyalty i can respect that. Third period was a bit easier to focus which worked out because i had a huge test in that class that i needed to focus on and if she was back and in that class i know i would be screwed.

It was time for my favorite class of all, Lunch. I walked into the Lunch room grabbed my food and went to our usual table in the back corner. Mike, Ty, and myself were talking about tonights fight when the whole room went dead silent when we hear a shout.

"WHAT THE FUCK!"a very familiar yet pissed off voice rang through the cafeteria making me jerk my head to where the voice came from and my eyes widen at what i saw, Jay standing in the middle of the room soaking wet looking more deadly then anyone I've seen before and Beth standing a couple feet away with an empty water bottle in her hands smirking...uh oh.

"Now that i have your attention i will say this one last time... Back off Caiden he is so not gonna end up with you!" Beth spat at her and i jumped up and tried to get to them but before i got halfway there Jay had delivered a descent right hook to beth making her fall on the floor clutching her jaw crying out and Matty (Beth's follower) tried what i think was to hit Jay but it was quickly dodged and

jay gave her a gut punch followed by swiftly jerking her knee up catching Matty's nose as she fell to the ground. I watched as Jay ran out of here and i was just stuck, who was this girl? So much for me getting her out of my head. The rest of the day went about as well as expected, my head was screwed and there was no way i was focusing on any of my schoolwork.

I was upstairs in my room when i heard the doorbell ring it had to be Mike and Ty ready for the fight. I grabbed my phone and headed downstairs, my mom had already let them in and they were talking at the door.

"So what are you boys getting into tonight?" She asked as she picked up May who was wrapped around her legs.

"Not to much." Mike answered giving her a smile. she turned and faced me with a knowing smirk " Uh huh just don't do anything stupid and get caught. come on May its bath time." She smiled and took May upstairs with her.

"Let's go." i said walking towards my car. On the way over there Tyler was driving us insane as he changed the song for the eighth time claiming each was better then the last but not listening to them fully.

"Dude! give it back!" Tyler yelled as he reached for his phone that Mike now had.

"I want to listen to one freaking song all the way through without your bipolar ass changing it!" Mike snapped back making Ty shrug and snatch his phone back.

"Fine hook your phone up then." Ty said sliding his phone back in his pocket. We arrived at the arena and it was just about to start.

As we made our way in the building it was ridiculously packed and loud as hell. We made our way through the crowd and sat close to, what we call, the pit as the announcer circles it. He was pretty tall and medium build with some messy Blonde hair, looked to be in his mid thirtys maybe.

"LADDDY'S AND GENTALMEN DO I HAVE A TREAT FOR YOU ALL TONIGHT!" The announcer yelled making everybody quiet down and turn all eyes on him.

"I HAVE BROUGHT MY VERY OWN WORLD WIDE CHAMPION TO FACE YOUR VERY OWN CHAMP BRUTE THE BRUUUUTTAAALLL!!!" He yelled pointing to Brute who was now in the corner of the ring holding his fists up as the crowd cheered his name.

"NOW GIVE A WARM WELCOME TO THE FIGHTER KNOWN BY MOST OF THE WORLD, MY CHAMPION DEEEEMMMMOOONNN!!!!" The announcer rawred making the crowd loose control as Demon came walking to the ring. I could not believe this, i have watched a few of this fighters fights and what makes Demon so much more mysterious was that demon was a woman, an undefeated woman. i watched as she circles the stage before stoping on her corner.

"Poor chicks gonna get her ass kicked." i looked at mike when he said this and swore i saw pity in his eyes but turned to look at the stage. both of the fighters were stripping off their jackets before throwing them into the crowd. It was usual for this to happen, the announcer makes sure to keep an eye on the fighters property and whoever catches them gets to meet the fighter after the fight. i watched as a tall beefy man caught brutes jacket and started cheering. I was about to turn back to the stage when i felt leather hit my chest i instantly grab onto it out of instinct and look down to see a big capital red D surrounded by flames, oh shit.

"You got Demons jacket you ass!" Mike said slapping my shoulder making me chuckle. I looked back at the stage and Brute was stretching and getting ready while Demon on the other hand wasn't moving a muscle, she was just staring at Brute studying him as if looking for something. After a few seconds she smirked and looked away starting to stretch.

"REMEMBER THIS IS THE UNDERGROUND SO YOU EITHER PASS OUT OR TAP OUT. READY...STEADY...FIIIGGHHTT!!" The announcer yelled.

CHAPTER 2: INTRODUCING DEMON

JAY'S P.O.V.

"NOW GIVE A WARM WELCOME TO THE FIGHTER KNOWN BY MOST OF THE WORLD, MY CHAMPION DEEEEMMMMOOONNN!!!!" I listened to the crowd scream my name when Xaiver announced i was fighting. I walked straight to the mat and climbed in not taking my eyes off brute, i circled a couple times before stopping in my corner to study Brute while he stretches in his corner. come on come on i cant find it, i looked as hard as i could, searching for any sign of a weak point. Just as i was about to give up and devise a new plan to win i saw it...he went to stretch his right leg as tight as he could then grabbed his left leg but grimaced as he stretched it only half as much as the right....Gotcha. i looked away with a smirk and stretched a little myself, we both took off our jackets and tossed them into the crowd for someone to hold during the fight. This was usual for underground fights, X keeps up with whoever gets my jacket so it doesn't get stole again.

"REMEMBER THIS IS THE UNDERGROUND SO YOU EITHER PASS OUT OR TAP OUT. READY...STEADY...FIIIGGHHTT!!"
X yelled as he backed out of the ring, brute and i circled it waiting for the other to make a move.
' Be patient ' I told myself ' stick to the plan' i continued as i waited for him to make a move.
He suddenly rushes at me swinging his fist at me putting all his weight into it, just as i was hoping he would.
I slid a step back missing his fist by an inch and using his weight against him i swung a punch landing
it on his right cheek as his body turned left from the force he put into his failed punch causing my punch to have twice the affect. He fell to his knee clutching his jaw as i swiftly did my signature and jerked my knee up and connected with his nose as hard as i can and enjoyed the cracking sound of his nose being crushed against my knee and he fell back blood rushing from his face and he was completely unconscious.
Xaiver grabbed my wrist and raised it high in the air as the crowd roared when X announced
"YOUR WINNER, NEW CHAMPION, AND MY GIRL DEEEEMMMOOONNN WINNER BY KNOCKOUT AFTER TWO MINUTES AND FIFTY-NINE SECONDS!!!"
I gave the crowd a nod then headed to my dressing room not bothering giving the crowd another glance.
After a few minutes i heard some voices from behind the door behind me and i knew it had to be X bringing
my jacket and the person who caught it. You see whoever catches the jacket gets to meet the fighter after
the fight...kinda tradition. I heard the door open up along with footsteps following, i smirked to myself before saying

"So how did you like the show?" as i asked i turned around to face X and whoever caught my jacket and i instantly tensed up but quickly relaxed as i remembered i had my face covered. Right next to Xaiver was a tall guy with a muscular build and black hair, a guy a little shorter with blonde hair and smaller build though he looks a lot like the tall guy, and Caiden.

"That was so awesome!" the shorter guy with blonde hair said with a huge smile on his face.

"Yea you kicked his ass! kinda surprised me." The tall guy with dark hair chuckled and rubbed the back of his neck.
i gave them both a simple smile and nodded. I became uneasy as i looked in caidens direction catching his icey blue
eyes right on me and he is hard in thought but not saying a word.

I put on my best smile and walked a couple feet forward and stopped a foot from Caiden, i was close enough i could
smell his cologne and it made that extremely unwelcomed wanting feeling in the pit of my stomach return.

"Can i have that back?" i asked in a very polite but quiet voice as i reached out my hand for my jacket and locked my eyes onto his.

"Jay..." he whispered almost to low for anyone to hear it, almost. I sighed taking a step back and pulled out a wet wipe wiping the paint off my face and taking the mask off as the boys just watched jaw dropped.

"Well fuck." i said as i turned and looked at all of them knowing there was no point denying it.
I can not explain it but something inside me was pulling for me to trust them
but i barley knew them it didn't make any sense.

"Oh shit..." The blonde said jaw dropped

"That make so much sense. " the tall guy mumbled

"So come on what was it? what gave me away?" i asked Caiden truly wanting to know so i don't make the same fuck up and Marcus finds me.

"Your eyes." He said looking at me as if in a daze and it took me back a bit i really wasn't expecting such a sweet answer. i swallowed hard not sure what to say back to that as we just stared into each others eyes, lost in a sea of ice i finally snapped outta my trance when i heard Xaiver slam the door shut and punch the door.

"SHIT!" He yelled as he punched the wall leaving a big dent in it and making the boys jump.

"Xaiver chill!" i gave him a warning look because i knew where this was going and needed him to be calm.

"You want me to chill!? Thanks to this Genius over here your officially not safe demon. First Raider found you, now this pretty boy goes and figure's out your identity. You cant stay here i think its best we get ahead of this before..." At this point X was ranting and was making my head spin so i cut him off mid sentence.

"X stop! you need to calm down alright. i am sure these boys wouldn't mind keeping their mouths shut about who i really am in exchange for something, Money is good doing what i do so you name it and its yours...take a little bit to decide what you want just please don't talk about me to anyone...don't let my identity get out?" i looked at them whole heartedly practically begging. They all look at each other then nodded before returning their gazes to me.

"We got you." The tall guy said " im mike and that's my brother Tyler... if im correct then you already know Caiden." He said with a smirk nodding his head toward Caiden.

i glanced his way and his eyes were locked on me and it made a shiver run up my spine.
i nodded once and looked at X.

"Now relax, im fine...its ok." i walked up to him and in a low voice i said " im safe x."
and i smiled giving him a reassuring hug and was happy when he relaxed a little.
" First sign of trouble and i promise im coming straight to you then im outta here okay?"
i looked him in the eyes and waited as he locked his eyes with mine and looked as if he was searching to make sure im being honest. he gives me a nod with a small smile.

"Alright i gotta go get ready for...A meeting but ill catch up with you guys tomorrow about what you want out of your end of the deal." i said to the boys as i walked past them grabbing my jacket from Caiden and headed down the hall.

"Demon...Please be careful and at the first sight of trouble you scream as loud as you can and im there." X called after me making me stop and turn around. i gave him a serious look then a simple nod before heading to the training room to put my jacket up then go ahead home before Raider pops up...maybe he was bluffing?

I opened my locker in the gym and put my jacket in it before locking it and turning around only to be pinned into the locker with rough hands holding me tight against the lockers. I looked up and lost my breath when met with the same hazel eyes that use to make me feel alive...Raider.

"Miss me love?" He asked leaning closer and i could feel his breath on my neck.
i quickly headbutted him and tried to get away when he stumbled back but i didn't get far when i felt a hand on my shoulder and i was slammed back into the lockers,

pinned once again by raider.

"Now there's my little firecracker." he smirked at me and i tensed at his nickname for me, it use to make me smile but now it only hurts.

"Get the HELL off of me!" i spat at him struggling against his hold.

"Now now, i know i messed up babygirl but i learned my lesson, i need you back baby." He said almost sounding truthfull but he always does.

"i said GET THE HELL OFF OF MEE!!!" i roared praying to God X is close enough to hear me.

"SHH love wouldn't want to be interrupted before we talked would you?" he said as he put his hand over my mouth to quiet me.

"GET YOUR HAND OFF HER NOW!!" a voice that made my stomach burn with desire roared making Raider let go of me and spin around in surprice at the interruption only to see Caiden, Mike, and Tyler standing at the doors fists clenched with Xaiver behind them as his eyes searches me from head to toe to make sure im not physically harmed. I used this as my opportunity to get away and ran straight behind the boys and into xaivers arms. ' don't cry, don't cry, don't cry' i repeatedly thought to myself almost shaking.

"Now who do we have hear?" Raider said with a smirk as he eyed up Caiden, Mike, and Tyler.

"Her family and you are?" Mike shot back looking like he was ready to loose it.

"you see im not a fan of being lied to and i happen to know for a fact that my little firecracker has no family and I am raider, her one and only." he winked at me when he said the last part. I didn't miss Caiden stiffen up when he said it to.

"That's where your wrong, Blood don't make you family." Ty shot back making me want to smile.

"You know damn well she isn't your anything!" Xaiver roared ready to kill raider.

"Jay, come back...please. we were unstoppable inside and outside of that ring.
i shouldn't have slept with that girl, i know i messed up now." Raider said as he locked his eyes on mine

" Its time for you to leave." Caiden said his words laced in venom.

Listen here this is between me and demon, so stay out of it prince charming."
Raider spat at him getting annoyed. i could tell this was going to be bad if i didn't do something fast.

"ENOUGH!!"I yelled as i wiggled out of Xaiver's arms and walked around the boys and toward's Raider as his eyes were locked on my every move. i stopped right infront on him keeping my gaze cold. i didn't miss how the boys were right behind me just in case

"I am tired, hungry and in pain. i have had a shitty day and want to go home so lets settle this the one way we know best, six months from Thursday, me and you fight in the championship. you win i come back, i win you leave and never say my name or show your face again." i growled at him letting the venom roll off each word. he looked at me hard for a minute then smiled "As you wish my little firecracker."
he tried to lean down and kiss me but i felt an arm snake around my waist and Caiden

pulled me behind him and the boys as they formed a protective stance around me.

"Till we meet again my love." Raider nodded at me before turning to walk out...Great.

CAIDEN'S P.O.V.

I couldn't believe it. I seriously could not process what was going on. Jay is Demon, the world wide underground fighter demon, the women who just took down brute. I watch as Jay tries to calm Xaiver.

"Now relax, im fine...its ok." She walked up to him and in a low voice she said " im safe x." and she smiled giving him a reassuring hug, they must be close. " First sign of trouble and i promise im coming straight to you then im outta here okay?" what trouble could she be talking about and what did she mean by the first sign of trouble? what trouble? all these thoughts were swarming through my mind that I hadn't noticed when she walked past us and grabbed her jacket from me and I watched as she walked down the hall.

"Demon...Please be careful and at the first sight of trouble you scream as loud as you can and im there." Xavier called to jay as she walked down the hall, she stopped and looked back at him giving a nod before disappearing through the doors to the locker room.

"Let me make something clear" Xaiver said calmly but words laced with silent threats. " Nobody needs to find out who she is, and if she is found because of you three I will make you suffer from a pain you have never experienced before. She has been through more then most of your nightmares, she is like my daughter and ill die before they get her again. She isn't safe, I doubt she'll ever be, do not walk into her life if you plan

on walking out because it will break her more then she already is and I will in return break you. with that being said...enter her life with caution...if you make a stand in her life you are all putting yourselves in danger and I can not promise you to survive but, I can promise that if she lets you in then she will do everything in her power to make sure you do."
he finished up his speech looking at us but letting his words really sink in.

"what happens if we walk away?" mike asked making my jaw clench. not because I was upset at him even thinking that after knowing she is in this much danger but because as much as my history has proved im best at staying out of peoples issues I don't see a reality where I can walk away from this, from her. Xaiver was about to say something when a voice ripped through the building halls that made us all take off towards the lockers.

"GET THE HELL OFF OF MEE!!!" jays voice thundered through the halls. I burst through the door

with Mike and Tyler right next to me and Xaiver right behind us. what I saw when I got in there made my blood boil, Jay was pinned to the lockers by some tall guy with dark brown hair and before I knew it the words roared out of my mouth.

"GET YOUR HAND OFF HER NOW!!" I yelled with clench fists. he obviously didn't expect the interruption because he let her go and swung around now facing up. I noticed jay used this time to get away and was in Xaivers arms.

"Now who do we have hear?" Raider said with a smirk as he eyed us up and down.

"Her family and you are?" Mike shot back looking like he was ready to loose it. Its rare for mike to put himself out for anyone other then me and ty, but I didn't let my shock divert my cold glare on raider.

"you see im not a fan of being lied to and i happen to know for a fact that my little firecracker has no family and I am raider, her one and only." he winked at Jay when he said the last part. I couldn't help but stiffen when he called her his. what does he mean no family?

"That's where your wrong, Blood don't make you family." Ty shot back surprising us all. Ty was the quiet type and definitely not the type to join in on conflict if he doesn't need to.

"You know damn well she isn't your anything!" Xaiver roared ready to kill raider.

"Jay, come back...please. we were unstoppable inside and outside of that ring. i shouldn't have slept with that girl, i know i messed up now." Raider said as he locked his eyes on Jay

" Its time for you to leave." I spat with my words laced in venom.

"Listen here this is between me and demon, so stay out of it prince charming. " Raider spat at me getting annoyed. I was getting ready to loose it myself.

"ENOUGH!!"Jay yelled as she wiggled out of Xaiver's arms and walked around us and toward Raider as his eyes were locked on her every move. She stopped right infront on him keeping her gaze cold. The boy's and i were right behind her just in case he tried anything.

"I am tired, hungry and in pain. i have had a shitty day and want to go home so lets settle this the one way we know best, six months from Thursday, me and you fight in

the championship. you win i come back, i win you leave and never say my name or show your face again."
she growled at him letting the venom roll off each word. he looked at her hard for a minute then smiled "As you wish my little firecracker." he tried to lean down and kiss her but no way in hell was i just going to let that happen. i wrapped my arm around her waist and pulled her behind us earning a steady glare from raider and i just smirked at him as if saying to try it.

"Till we meet again my love." Raider nodded at her before turning to walk out...what a dick i thought. the second he is gone i turn and face jay who was once again in Xaivers arms.

" I'm fine X, everythings fine. Raider is the least of my worries." jay says trying to reassure him as she pulls away and turns to face us.

" it is late and im sure you all need to get home, i don't want you guys to get into any trouble. we can talk tomorrow if that's better." she said calmly looking at us. i glance at the boys who instantly look uncomfortable and sad...she didn't know.

" Did i say something wrong?" she asked noticing the change in their energy.

"No you didn't its just..." Ty started looking over at mike as if asking how to say it.

"Me and Ty don't have a home. its a long story but nobody is waiting on us where we stay."
Mike says finishing Ty's sentence. when they were young there mother passed, a couple years later there father just vanished. Nobody knows what happened to him but since they are 18 they were on their own.

" And you?" she asked looking directly at me as if she didn't hear what they just said.

"Its me, my mom, and sister but i don't need to be home at any certain time." i said trying not to acknowledge the growing pull deep in my gut as i stare into her evergreen eyes with golden flecks like fire swimming through them.

" Alright then come with me to my place and we can talk there." she said giving Xaiver a last smile and walking towards the exit. i looked at the boys who just shrugged and walked after her, when we got outside she was standing next to a gorgeous 67 Chevy impala waiting for us.

"This your ride?" i asked walking up to her eyeing every inch of that beauty... the car i mean i have done eyed her since day one.

"This is my livelihood....my joy...my beast." She said smiling and an actual smile that reached her eyes making her shine. "You three follow me if you can keep up." she smirked at us as she climbed into her car and smiling another one of those perfect smiles as the engine roars to life. I got to admit if i had a type of girl i could see being with she definitely fits the bill.

After following her for a little bit we ended up in the middle of nowhere surrounded by fields of trees. We follow her through a old road passing through the trees till we arrive at a empty field with a single two story house sitting in the back left corner. we pulled in next to her and got out examining her home... it was beautiful, peaceful, and private.

"you boy's going to stand there all night or gonna come inside?" She asked already

walking through the front door leaving it open behind her for us to follow him.

JAY'S P.O.V.

I walked down the hall hearing the boys right behind me as i walked towards my back porch. i flipped on the lights and grabbed four beers and handed three of them to the boys before sitting down on the patio couch out back. we sat there in peaceful silence as they observed my yard in awe and i couldn't help but smile. It was indeed nice, it had a pool which i use to do laps in every night before bed but probably wouldn't tonight. it was an open back yard in the field surrounded by trees. I have furniture and a tv outside as well as a grill and mini fridge. i have to say when x set this up for me he didn't miss a beat, it was breath taking.

"It's a beautiful home, what do your parents do for a living?" Ty asked looking at him. I looked at him and gave him a small smile before looking out at the tree line.

"Look i completely get your trying to get conversation flowing but there's something we all need to clarify. Nobody but X and unfortunately Raider knows shit about me. i do not open up to people because it isn't safe and when i say it isn't safe i don't just mean for you i mean for ME." i said verifying the ME part as i looked at each one of them in the eye's landing my eyes on Caiden. " If i let you in, and you are put in danger...then i officially have a weak point in my life and if i let you in" i said finally removing my eyes from Caidens and looked back out to the woods. " then you walk out ill be at risk of being caught and killed or used because of being distracted by my pain. do you understand what im saying?" i asked not looking at them

"You can trust us jay... we don't ever put ourselves out there to help anyone but something

about you is different...we want to be there for you and can handle whatever comes our way."
i heard Caiden say and when i looked into his icey blue eyes i noticed they turned a stormy blue showing complete seriousness, i looked over at mike and ty to see them nodding in agreement. i did something i have never done before in that moment right there, i let the tears that have been held prisoner in my eyes win against me and a single tear rolled down each side of my face and i took a deep breath turning my gaze from them and back to the trees once again.

"My father was killed when i was eight and then my mother died when i was nine, this house is my own i have been saving up as much as i could when i started fighting for myself, i gave what i could to X as i bounced from state to state. He had this place built to my exact specifications, has a pool for training, a home gym, three bedrooms and three bathrooms and my favorite part is its private." i said answering Tylers question from earlier.

"Damn" Caiden said looking at me with pain in his eyes.

"What happened after they passed." Mike asked making me tense, i haven't really talked about it to anyone other then X and raider and im honestly to tired to make something up.

i took a deep breath trying to steady my heartrate which i was sure Caiden could here by the way he tensed up as was glaring at mike. he reached over and grabbed my hand making shocks run through it and heat rise up my arm. i was surprised at first but relaxed because honestly i could use the comfort.

"its a long story but the short version is that i was held captive till i turned fourteen and escaped, Xaiver or X for short always took care of me when i was held captive there, bandaged me up and helped me train and become stronger. he is the reason i escaped and everytime they get close to finding me or when they find me he gets me out in the nic of time.... i would probably be dead if it wasn't for him." i said as i smiled to myself. I cleared my throat and stodd up taking my hand off caidens instantly missing his warmth.

"Its late, ill show you to the guest rooms and we should all get some rest. follow me." i said to them as i walked inside towards the stairs. they followed me upstairs and to the rooms. theirs were side by side and across from mine.

"Woah." Mike said as he walked into the room with tyler. it wasn't anything to fancy, it has a big king size bed and a flat screen tv, with a walkin closet and a balcony. I left them to there room and showed Caiden to his, right next door. It was the exact same as the other room.

"Have a good night. bathrooms down the hall and to the left and if you need anything im right across the hall." i smiled at him as he takes in the room.

"Thank you jay. Are you ok...after tonight?" he asked looking at me stepping closer to me placing his hand on my arm letting his thumb rub circles on my skin. Sparks shot out just from his touch making my heart pound.

"I don't think i have processed it yet to be honest but im also exhausted, but if not i will be." I answered trying to ignore the fact that we are close enough for me to feel his warm minty breath hitting my cheek. he looked at me hard before his eyes flicked to my lips then back up to my eyes. Was he thinking about kissing me? No he couldn't be? Could he? i stood there for a minute to long not sure what to do when he started leaning a little closer, like i was sprayed with cold water i jumped backwards.

"Have a good night Caiden." i said and walked out of the room leaving him standing there with a shocked expression on his face. everything in me tells me to trust them but what i feel around Caiden is a whole nother level, one that i can't allow into my life, i cant be weak right now. i jumped in the shower and let the hot water wash todays events away.

Raider here and attacking me, My identity blown, fight at school which means attention drawn, caidens sudden interest in me and those damn sparks. i haven't felt that before and its fucking scary. Those damn eyes that i could get lost in and that hair that im drawn to tangle my fingers through. ugh i found myself getting more stressed then before and decided to get out of the shower and get to bed. i plugged up my phone and layed down, checking the time before i went to bed it was right at midnight. i closed my eye and felt the darkness overtake me.

â€¦

I jolted awake in my bed almost hyperventilating and shaking pouring sweat all over my body, it was just a night mare, it was just a night mare i repeatedly reassured myself. i have never been this scared in my life and that's saying something, usually my nightmares are memories but this was different, this was officially my biggest fear and it is so capable of coming true and that's what scares me the most. looking at the time it was right at four a.m once again and i refused to go back to sleep after that dream. i got out of bed and crept down to the gym being sure not to wake the boys.

After bandaging my hands and putting my headphones in i started to take it all out on the punching bag.

CHAPTER 3: ME CASA SU CASA

CAIDEN'S P.O.V.

I layed here in the worlds softest bed feeling like the worlds most dumbfounded dumbass. I do not understand what I did wrong, I don't understand why she pulled away from me. Stuff like this hasn't happened to me before I never have a problem with women's but jay... I have never wanted to be with someone as much as I want to be with her yet she acts like im going to murder her. im not gonna give up though there has got to be a way to get her to let me in. I think about the events from today and my heart clenches for jay, she has nobody and she is being hunted yet here she is as strong as ever.

It's about one in the morning and I could feel myself dozing off with Jay on my mind. I woke up to my alarm on my phone going off telling me that my peace and quiet for the day was over with. I silenced my phone and starting dozing back off when suddenly the thoughts from yesterday rushed into my mind and jerked myself straight up remembering im in Jays home and I tried to kiss her last night but she ran off. Just then the door opened and mike and tyler came walking in.

"Bro I haven't slept that hard in a long time." Mike said walking up to me.

"Right I didn't even know a bed could be that comfortable." Tyler said walking up behind mike

"Yea this place is nice. you guys see if Jay was up yet?" I asked them standing up from the bed. They both shook there head no smirking at me

"Oh shut it!" I huffed at them before walking out of the room and towards jay's. The door was open but when I peaked in she wasn't in there. I fought ever urge I had to snoop through her room to get to know her better partly because the guys would pick at me but mostly because im 100% sure she would kick my ass.

"Sounds like she's in the gym Bro." Mike called down the hall and we headed towards the noise. Walking in I saw a very breath taking view. Jay was punching the bags so fast and hard that you'd think she was extremely focused yet she was completely zoned out. she was sweating like hell which only made her more attractive. She had her headphones in so couldn't hear when we called her name, she just punched again and again, harder and harder. I reached over and flickered the lights off and on making her jump a little before looking our way.

"Shit im sorry did I wake you guys up? I tried to be quiet." She said as she took off her headphones walking up to us breathing hard. How long had she been in here.

" No...it's seven in the morning. our alarms went off for school." I answered slowly as she gave me a surprised look.

"I guess I lost track of time. There's food in the kitchen you can help yourselves im gonna go jump in the shower." she smiled at us pointing out the kitchen as she went upstairs.

I walked to her fridge and saw it was well packed of food. I decided it would be nice to cook her breakfast as a thank you for letting us crash here. The boys were on the couch playing call of duty while I finished cooking the bacon.

I was making the last plate adding eggs, bacon, stir fried potato's and sat it at the table.

"Wow what's all this? Smell's great!" Jay said as she rounded the corner.

"just a small thank you for letting us crash here, it made the guy's night. Also an im sorry for last night I went to far with you." I said sending her a sincere smile.

"It's fine you didn't do anything wrong, Just got wrapped up in the moment." she smiled at me, if only she really knew.

"You so Cheated you shot me in the back!!!" mike yelled stomping into the kitchen with tyler behind him laughing hysterically.

"Your such a sore loser Bro!!" Ty laughed at him earning him a glare from mike

"You kept shooting me in the back!" Mike yelled

"Hey I would rather shoot my enemy in the back then have them see me coming and kill me." Jay said as she sat down and dug into her food. I couldn't help but smile at her, she was pretty smart. That shut them up as they sat at the table and started eating.

"So Mike and Tyler I have been thinking." Jay said looking at them making both of them look up at her with anticipation in there eyes not sure what she was going to say.

"If we are gonna do this talking about my life thing then id like to know why you have no home." She stated making me jerk my head to them eyes wide. both of there jaws dropped not expecting this and she said it so calm like it was natural.

"UM..." Ty said not able to make his mouth spit out his words.

"Our dad died when we were young and our mom got into drugs really bad, wasn't safe to stay with her anymore so we bounce around but we manage because we have each other." Mike spoke up knowing it's easier for him to talk about it then it is for Tyler. She looked at them both intently before clearing her throat.

" Have either of you put any thought into what you want for staying quiet about who and where I am?" she asked not taking her eyes off them while my eyes were glued on her. They looked at each other and nodded then looked back at her.

"We don't want anything." Ty said

"We will keep you safe without you having to bribe us." Mike finished sternly. she gave them another long intent gaze before drinking some juice.

"This is a five bedroom house and its only me here, you boys have no home and I would really like it if you stayed here and make it into your homes as well." She said calmly taking another bite of her food and made my mouth drop this time. She was giving them a home, somewhere safe and warm with food and somebody to care if they show up at night or not. I looked over at them and there were tears streaming down their faces as their eyes were looked on her. They both stood up and walked over to her slowly dropping down to their knees both on opposite sides of her and engulfed her in a hug as they started to cry.

"Thank you...thank you so fucking much." Mike cried into her lap as tyler remained speechless crying into her shoulder.

"Don't thank me mike....It's time I let myself have a family to have my back...its time I come out of my darkness that I have carried for so long. you boys deserve joy and peace not constant fear and pain," She said choking back her tears but they were forming in her eyes.

JAY'S P.O.V.

My heart ached as I held Mike and Tyler while they cried muffled thank you's. I knew I could thrust them, we were a lot alike and have been through some of the same stuff.
I have such a big house and now I believe this is why, they need a home and im certain this is where they are suppose to be. I look up at Caiden who has a couple loose tears sliding down his face and over his lips. He was looking at me with a million emotions running on his face. We sat there for a long while when i noticed both boys have stopped crying and were relaxing.

"Come on your foods probably cold." i said as i nudged both of them with my arms.
They stood up not uttering a word and went back to their seats, i knew this meant more then i would ever know to them and they needed time for them to process what is going on.

"We should probably get going i have a test in chemistry today and can't afford to fail it." Caiden said breaking the silence. i looked up at him and nodded in agreement. Everybody keeps the silence as we got up from the table, i went and grabbed my stuff before heading out to my car.

"Mind if i ride with you?" i turn and see Tyler giving me a small smile and i smile back at him.

"Hop in" i say getting in and once again smiling bright when the engine roars to life.
We drove in comfortable silence before Tyler turned to look at me.

"I can tell you have been hurt by a lot of people so it makes me wonder why you trust us enough to give us a home with you, its more then a room to sleep in, its a spot in your life something that can't be easy to give." He asks looking at me sincerely. He's right it wasn't easy for me to let them it but it honestly shocked me when he said all this, from what i can tell Ty is quiet and i really didn't expect it out of him. i gave him a small glance and then looked back at the road.

"Besides X i learned that the only person i can truly trust 100% is myself and something deep inside screams for me to trust you three and that has never happened before so i know that i can trust it. i can trust you." i sighed and took a left taking the back road to school but ty didn't say anything just continued looking at me.

"When i was young i had a big brother, he was my best friend, my hero, my protector. He was my half brother, we had different dads, After my parents passed i was sent to live with him because he was seventeen and my only family." i paused trying to gather myself and force the pain out of my voice. " his father's name is Malcom and when he showed up with me Jake, my brother, threw me in the basement and my beatings started... never by jakes hand but he allowed it and didn't protect me." i felt a stray tear roll down my check because this was the first time i have talked about jakeâ€¦not even with raider.

"I truly believe that if i let you in then you wont hurt me â€¦ i miss having a brother anyways." i chuckled trying to ignore my anxiety roaring inside me. Tyler sat there silently as we pulled to the school parking lot and got out of the car Mike and Caiden were standing there waiting on us. The second i close my car door Tyler has me wrapped in a surprising but comforting hug and i return on to him. after a second he let go and looked me in the eyes...

"I got you sis." he whispered smiling and winked at me before we turn to Caiden and mike who were looking at us confusingly.

"Where did you guys go?" Caiden asked looking between the two of us.

"We just needed a second to talk." i smiled at Caiden and sent tyler a wink making him smile. mike and Caiden looked at each other confused before we heard the bell ring.

" Gotta get to gym." i said walking away from them.

"Wait you have gym too?" Caiden asked catching up to me.

"Yea but didn't know you were in it." i replied

"We all are." mike said as he caught up to us with tyler on his right.

"Cool." i chuckled walking towards gym class. I didn't miss all the stares and whispering as i walked through the halls with the "IT" boys, i smiled to myself. We got to gym and i saw Danny in the corner on his phone, i walked over to him and sat down.

"Hey danny." i said greeting him with a smile. He looked up with a smile but it dropped when he saw the boys with me.

"Uh hey jay..." He said giving me a forced smile back. i looked at the boys and nodded for them to leave and they did so, Caiden hesitated at first but Ty pulled on him to leave ...Already so Protective of me i smiled watching tyler then returned my attention to Danny just watching me hard.

"What?" i asked sounding annoyed but really wasn't.

"Oh don't you Dare what me" He glared at me.

"Well i guess we are all sort of friends now." i told him with a shrug as we started our laps.

"Friends? With them? are you trying to drive beth crazy?" he slightly chuckled at me. "They don't make friends outside themselves Jay." he stated

"Well they do now and i don't give a fuck about beth â€¦ ill crush her if i have to." i gave an evil smirk making him chuckle. We chatted for a while and i noticed the boys were right behind us the whole time. we joked back and forth before gym was over, i said goodbye to danny and started towards my locker .

" hey wanna walk to class with me?" i turned to see a smiling Caiden and i returned the smile as i closed my locker.

"Sure" i replied. we walked in comfortable silence but the smiles never leave our faces. we sat side by side in physics as we waited for class to start.

"What you did for mike and ty was unbelievably amazing...you have no clue what it means to them, to me angel." he smiled at me making me grin.

"It means just as much to me." i replied. i saw him scoot closer to me before tucking my hair behind my ear resting his hand on mine and i didn't move it off of me this time, we just stared into each others eyes until the teacher broke our gaze.

"Morning everyone, today we will be discussing...blah blah blah blah blah blah." she continued on while i felt my eyes getting heavy. i looked at Caiden whos eyes were locked on me still.

"Wake me when class is over please." i asked before laying my head down on the desk and drifted deep deep asleep.

â€¦

I look around and see im in a field, it looks weirdly familiar but before i even have time to look around im fozen, eyes locked on nun other then Marcus. i look to his right and see raider standing there shock in his eye that i had a hard time understanding why he looked like that. To Marcus's left is Jake and he is red as blood screaming and crying at marcus.

"No you said you wouldn't kill her!!! Put the gun down Marcus!!!" Jake roared at his father, i force my eyes to marcus and tense, he has a gun pointed right at me. I stand up straight and lock eyes with marcus.

"Shoot me... ill die before i let you take me back." i spat at him meaning every word. he looked shocked but then replaced it with a smirk that made my gut twist.

"Oh i figured as much but will you let him die?" Marcus asked smugly now pointing the gun

to my left, all color left my body im sure of it because right next to me was Caiden.
Just then i heard the hammer on the gun pull back and a shot rang through my ears everything now black.

â€¦

I jerk up with Caiden lightly shaking my shoulder. The sudden movement made Caiden take a step bad. i was breathing heavly and pouring sweat ' it was a dream' ' it was a dream' i continued to mentally tell myself.

"Hey hey are you ok angel?" Caiden asks cupping my face in his hands tilting my head up so my eyes meet his.

"Yea yea im fine im sorry just a nightmare, im good tho." i said sending him a reassuring smile and tho he looked as if he knew i wasn't telling him something but didn't mention it. He drops his hands from my face and grabs my bag for me.

"Let's go" he said walking towards the door and i just followed silently.

CAIDEN'S P.O.V.

I walked her to her locker and handed Jay her backpack before pulling out the paper i wrote my number on earlier holding it out to her.

"What's this?" she asked grabbing the paper.

"In case you wanna talk or need anything." i smiled walking away from her and heading to my Chemistry class, i Had a test today and being at the head of the class i usually finish it early as well as mike and tyler. When you are finished with your test your allowed to be dismissed for the rest of the period so i was looking forward to the free time. I walked into class and saw the boys had beat me there, i walked to the back and sat right in between mike and Tyler.

"Sup bro." mike said nodding his head acknowledging my presence, tyler looked up and nodded then looked back at his phone, thats it.

"Who have you been talking to bro, your constantly lost in your phone texting away not even seeing the world right in front of you?" i asked locking eyes with Tyler. His eyes grew slightly wide and his face paled as he slid his phone into his pocket.

"have not dude..." tyler said giving me a glare. fine we will talk about this alone later on.

"What did you and Jay talk about this morning?" i asked trying not to sound jealous but i simply had to know. He smirked at me before replying

"She told me she use to have a brother, but honestly i don't feel right telling you what all she told me, feels like i'd be betraying her trust and she said she is claiming me as her brother, if we are being perfectly honest i can see her as my sister and if she wants you to know she will tell you. you just need to ask her." Tyler finished looking a level of confident i have never seen before. i swear mike and i have had to look retarded with our jaws dropped and eyes buldged out. Tyler has barley ever said more then a couple words at a time let alone be so outspoken he is always quiet and keeps his answers shot but the way he is talking right now makes you believe he is the most confident man on earth.

"Quiet down class and clear your desks for the test." the teacher said walking into the room and snapping our gaze off of Tyler who was smiling proudly.

Soon finishing my test with still fifteen minutes left i gave it to the teacher and walked out of the classroom. I got into the hall and sat against my locker knowing in about five minutes the boys will be coming out of the room to meet up with me.

"Hey baby where have you been hiding?" i heard a nauseating voice come from my right, i huffed a deep breath and rolled my eyes before looking to meet eyes with beth.

"What do you want?" i said against gritted teethe

"Awe don't be like that babe, i miss you." She said trying to sound sweet but only made my skin crawl. she came to sit next to me and it made me jump up and on my feet in point two seconds.

"Fuck off beth, i want nothing to do with you." i spat at her hoping she would leave me be.

"You don't mean that, we are perfect together just hear me out." i was seriously about to explode at her but before i got the chance to i felt an are snake up my bicep sending sparks through my skin. i look over to see jay clutching to my arm and i swear she had to hear my heart pounding out of my chest right now.

"Hey babe, you wanna get outta here... you still owe me that date." she said to me making my stomach flip. she looks over at beth and glares at her making beth flinsh back a little.

"What!?" Jay said letting her voice hold straight power. beth stomped her foot before walking away angrily. i looked at jay who was trying so hard not to bust out laughing.

"Dude you should have seen your face!!! it was better then hers!!" she laughed now clutching her stomach doubling over.

"Oh shut it, you took me by surprise." i snarked at her but let a smirk come to my face.

"it looked like you needed some help." she said smiling now breathing heavily from all the laughing.

"i did thank you, that girl is nuts!" i said shaking my head. i noticed her hand was still wrapped around me forearm and i couldn't help but welcome her warmth, i looked down at her and couldn't help but take in that amazing smile. She stiffened and turned a shade of red before quickly letting go of my arm.

"Yea i kinda figured that out already." she said looking anywhere but at me still blushing and it made me smile, i loved seeing this side of her.

"Whats so funny?" I turned to see Tyler and mike coming up and tyler standing right beside jay when he gets here. her smile gets bigger when she see's him and my legs almost gave out at the sight.

"Oh my God you guys should have been here!!" She said starting to laugh again. Suddenly her phone went off and her whole vibe changed, she stood up straight and stiff. she tucked her phone into her pocket and then turned to face us, all of our smiles were gone in a blink. Jay stood there with fire in her eyes and back to her usual blank self, like a switch flipped and it made my heart clench for that bright eyed smile she had a second ago.

"Looks like im fighting tonight." she said giving no emotion at all, this was ridiculous i mean she fought and won against brute, was attacked by raider, looked as if she barley slept last night when we found her training this morning. i mean the women was exhausted.

"That doesn't sound like a good idea." I said trying not to sound to stern with her.

"Yea you look exhausted." Mike pitched in making me nod.

"Gee thanks asshats." She glared at them.

"What do you think?" She turned to face tyler with soft eyes and honestly made me wish i was on the receiving end of that look. Mike and i looked at tyler expecting him to back us but he just looked at her intently in her eyes.

"You good?" was all he asked her placing his hands on her shoulders. she smiled at him and nodded firmly and confidence was radiating off of her. he turned to face us saying

"Ok then shes got this, leave it be." he stated in a firmness he has never shown before, what the hell did they talk about earlier?

"But.." Mike started to argue but tyler stepped forward placing a hand on his brothers shoulder and giving him a hard stare. " If you want her to trust us then you need to trust her." he said making mike and i let out a sigh of defeat and nodding our heads. he stepped back next to her and went back to his usual self on his phone.

CHAPTER FOUR: RAFAL

JAY'S P.O.V.

I stood in the locker room with the guys trying to get ready for tonight's fight still. I haven't heard much about this fighter and i sat there watching a report of him online, he was a skilled fighter. He was tall and built as well as fast, he has been out of the ring for like a year now but im not quiet sure why. Besides that im stumped on any facts to help during this fight...it's going to be a tough one.

"Hey you got this, relax." i look over to see Caiden looking at me softly. i can't help but relax as places his hand on my knee and stare into his eyes...he feels safe.

"Yea just like being prepared." i say glancing to see mike and tyler sit next to me. Tyler looks a bit uneasy and its making me worry which is definitely not what i need tonight. i nudge him making him look at me.

"What's going on?" I ask locking eye's with me. He looks at me then at the others before shaking his head.

"Nothing." he said look at the table infront on us.

"Dude you have been off for a while now and we all noticed it." Mike said

"You can talk to us." Caiden added giving him a warm smile. Tyler looked at all of us hard still unsure of if he was going to say something i added in "Im not going to be able to focus tonight if you don't tell me whats bothering you, don't let me go into that ring distracted Ty." i gave him a sad smile before he sighed in defeat.

"I was going to tell you guys i swear i was but every time i came close i chickened out." he started looking directly at the ground " A couple years ago i relized that im gay but have been keeping it to myself." He paused letting that sink in as he slowly glanced up to look at everyone except mike.

"I wish you would have said something sooner bro, i would have stopped trying to set you up with chicks." Mike said slinging an arm around ty's shoulder making me smile. Ty let out a smile but it disappeared when he looked at me, he locked his eye's with mine and swallowed hard.

"There's more... a few month ago i met someone, that's who i have been texting so much, and i only recently found out he is a fighter as well, and a couple hours ago i found out that he's you competitor tonight jay." He's face was pale when he finished saying this and i couldnt't help it as i started laughing, he looked at me confused they all did actually.

"Just because we are fighting tonight does not mean we wont get along, on the mat we are competitors and i will give it my all but off the mat we are all fighters and deserve respect." i said smiling at them making Tyler smile big.

"Demon let's go your on." one of the stage guys nodded for me to follow.

"You got this D." Tyler said hugging me

"No hard feelings when i kick his ass alright?" i smirked at him he just chuckled and nodded.

"Be careful." I turned and looked at Caiden giving him a warm smile

"Now where's the fun in that." i smirked and walked out towards the mat.

"TONIGHT RAFAL IS CHALLENGING OUR VERY OWN CHAMPION DEEEMMOONN!!" The crowd roared
As i walked on the matt and went to my corner not taking my eyes off of him.
He was definitely taller in person, he smirked at me and nodded his head down
once as if saying hey, i returned the gesture. he does his stretches and unlike
with Brute i didn't see any weakness, the hard way it is.

"SAME RULES APPLY, TAP OUT OR BLACK OUT, READY, STEADY, FIGHT!!" X yelled sending
me a wink that made me smile. We circled the mat both having our guard up and eye's
locked on the other, he nodded and stepped forward attempting to land a right hook
that i dodged quickly hitting his gut. i took two steps back as he gets to his feet
and regained his stance he takes me by surprise kicking my gut hard enough for me
to buckle to a knee and he was behind me in a instant pulling my right arm between
my shoulder blades.

"Nice try." i mumbled to him before reaching up grabbing the back of his neck and
with all my force i curled forward slamming his body to the mat. i quickly staddle
him and land two blows to the jaw and one to the guy. he rolled over and pinned
me to the ground giving two jabs to my abdomen, ignoring the pain i swiftly
brought my legs up and wrapped them around his neck putting him in a chock hold.
I hold him tighter and tighter puling harder and harder till i feel him tapping
hard and fast on my thigh. i instantly let him go and jump up ignoring the shooting
pain coursing through my body which was getting very easy to do. i put on a blank

face and nodded to the crowd, i reached my hand out to rafal to help him up and he looked up at me and smiled taking my hand, i gave him stern nod but made sure he could see the small smile i gave him before turning and walking back stage.
" AND OUR CHAMPION REMAINS DEEMMMOOONN" X's voice boomed through the building making me smile.

I sat on the couch in my changing room and winced every time i breathed, i may be able to hide it for a minute but its still unreal. the door opened and i looked up to see Caiden.

"You ok?" he asked looking at me with concern in his eyes.

"Yea I've had worse." i smiled at him but he only deepened his from. "You should get to a doctor to be checked out." he said making me tense up but' i hissed in pain when i did. "NO!" i all but shouted i cleared my thoat and in a lower voice i corrected"no i can't, they found me because of that one time." i said shaking my head no over and over.

"ok ok, no hospital." he scooted closer and pulled me into a side hug.
" i got you angel" he whispered to me as he held me, after a minute all the pain was forgot about as my stomach did flips at Caiden being so close

"Wheres the boys?" i asked sitting up and pulling away from caidens warmth

"Tyler was going to come with me but mik kept pushing to meet raider, got to say i knew something was up with ty lately but didn't even think it could be something like this, im happy he finally said something though. this newfound

confidence in him is good on him and it has everything to do with you, thank you Jay." he said now sitting up his nose a breath away from mine now.
My breathe caught in my throat as i was trapped by his eyes, full of so much sincerity and passion, nobody has ever looked at me like that before.
"You are so amazing angel." he whispered and his menty breath hit me instantly.
His eyes flicked to my lips and he started leaning in slowly, this time i didn't move, i couldn't, i didn,t want to. Just as i feel his lips graze mine i hear the door open and i instantly jump back and Caiden pulled his arm away swearing "shit" under his breath.

Looking at the door i see X glaring at Caiden, mike and ty smirking at us, and Who i know as rafal standing next to ty smiling at me. "Not a word." i glared still clutching my side from when i jumped up earlier, Rafal's smile faded as he eyed my hand on my stomach and walking up to me. he stops right infront of me and stops locking eyes with mine.

"Didn't mean to go that hard on you, one i was really trying for that title for my comeback fight and two i wanted to impress ty and his family." he smiled widely holding out his hand to me and i couldn't help but smile as i took his hand shaking it.

"Your a fighter, no matter who you step in that ring with you fight, you give it everything in you, and even if you loose... you win." i said as his smile brightened. Ty came up and hug me as did mike

"Nice moves tonight." mike said hugging me

"Yea i knew you could do it." Tyler asked. i took a deep breath and looked around the room

"Let's go home. you can come hangout if you want Rafal." I said making everyone smile.

TYLERS P.O.V.

It was about Nine thirty and everyone was in the living room of Jays home...our home.
I still couldn't believe it, mike and i have a home because of Jay. That girl has been through hell and back and decides to invite us into her home, into her life.
I watched as she laughed at mike getting mad as she beat him on the racing game.
He was a sore loser for sure. Mike gave up and went to the kitchen probably for more pizza, and Caiden slid right into his seat beside her not missing a beat and smiled at her making her face redden as she clutched her controller. Oh they are so into eachother, being the quiet one has its perks like noticing the things nobody else does.

"Ready to loose angel?" he smiled at her making her give him a wicked smirk

"Bring it pretty boy." she smirked and his smile grew

"So you think im pretty huh? damn i was hoping for sexy." he fake hurt in his voice clutching his chest. i rolled my eyes

"Oh shut up and play." she glared at him. he smiled and grabbed the remote and started playing, i glance over at the kitchen to see mike and Rafal eating pizza and laughing as they talk. i smiled to myself i like that they were getting along. I stood up and started walking towards the kitchen.

"You guys save me any or eat it all?" i asked walking to a now empty pizza box. Mike and Rafal smirk at the shocked look on my face.

"You evil animals!" i glared at them making them smile more. Rafal stands up and walks to the microwave opening it pulling out a plate with two slices of pizzas and handing them to me.

"Don't scare me like that!" i glared at him but felt the smirk on my face. he just smiled in return.

"I should probably get home, its getting late and i need to get back to my place before my mom kills me." Rafal laughs as he give Mike a bro hug and turns hugging me.

"Ill text you when im home." he smiled at me making me grin.

"Sounds good." i said. He walked into the living room and said his goodbyes to Caiden and Jay before leaving. i finished a slice of pizza then returned to the living room carrying the other slice and handing it to jay, she took it happily.

"They ate all the rest and i figured you were still hungry." i chuckled as she bit into the pizza and nodded up and down.

"thank you!" she smiled at me. mike followed in behind me only seconds after i sat down.

"Rafal if pretty cool bro i like him." Mike said to me as he took a seat.

"Yea and he seems nice." Caiden added in with a nod.

"Dude can fight too." Jay said in between bites of pizza. i couldn't help but smile, she looked like a chipmonk.

"Glad yall approve." i told them smiling. I look around and feel the warmth burn within me, this is my family, these are my people. My eyes lock on jays smiling face and bright eyes, and i will protect them.

CAIDEN'S P.O.V.

It was getting late and jay was passed out on the couch sound asleep. I looked over at tyler who was texting, probably Rafal. I was glad to know what was going on with him, and to know he was happy.

"hey" i whispered at Tyler to get his attention. He looked up at me then down at Jay.

"im gonna take her to her room. be right back." i whispered to him and he looked at me for a second and then nodded looking back down to his phone. sheesh no trusting ass. I gently scooped her up and headed towards her room, i stopped in the doorway when she started to wiggle but calmed down snuggled into my chest. If i didn't calm my heartrate down it was probably going to wake her up but the way she snuggled into my chest was driving me insane. I walked over to her bed and layed her down covering her up with a throw blanket on her bed. i headed out of her room but stopped when i saw a single picture on her wall next to the door. Its had a women and man laughing in it with what looks like jay around six or seven giggling and holding her was a teenage boy smiling so big. That must have been her family, they looked happy. Tyler said something about her having a brother, wonder what happened to him?

i walked out of her room closing the door quietly behind me and walking back down stairs.

"Hey bro i got to get home i haven't seen them since last night and wanna check in but ill see you guys at school." i told tyler as i got down stairs.

"Alright ill see you tomorrow. ill tell mike when he gets up in the morning." he said as i walked towards the door.

Getting home it was ten p.m and by now may is usually asleep and mom is having what she calls "Me time". i walked inside and was almost tackled by a very loud may

"Caiden!!!" she yelled " you have been gone forevers!" she pouted as she stuck out that bottom lip making me pick her up.

"Aww im sorry sweety what are you doing up?" i asked her giving her a hug.

"She wanted her big brother to tell her goodnight and refused sleep until you got home... you sir owe me 'me time'" my mom said walking up to us making me smile.

"You got it mom." after a few minutes of stuggling i finally got may to go to bed but its going to cost me extra ice cream. i walked into the kitchen to get moms questions over with.

"Go ahead and ask." i said making her smile, not even trying to hide it.

"So who's the girl?" she asked doing that weird eyebrow thing wiggleing them up and down.

"yes mom im good thanks for asking, no nothing new going on with me. but thanks for asking" i smirked at her making her laugh.

"Fine don't tell me about her but maybe at least tell me her name?" she asked giving me big hopeful eyes.

"Jay" i said smiling from ear to ear

"Enough said" she smirked looking at me grinning ear to ear. We talked for a little but then i headed to my room to get some sleep. i decided before falling asleep that tomorrow i was going to ask jay if she would be willing to talk to me a little bit about her story, i want to hear it and i want to get to know her better.

i woke up to my phone going off telling me it was time for school but this time when i got out of bed i was energetic and excited to get to school, i wanted to see jay and im not ashamed to admit it. I went downstairs and told my mom and May goodbye before heading to school. when i pulled up Jay's car was already there and i parked right next to it. I walked up to the school and through the halls when i froze in my tracks, jay was pinned against the lockers by some guy i haven't met before. I was about to get him off of her when out of nowhere a deadly looking Tyler rips him off of her and has him pinned on the floor punching him over and over again with so much rage i actually debated trying to get in his way, quiet small tylers way. I shook it off and tried to pull him off but he pushed me off with a force i didn't know he had and he was back on top of this man hitting him again and again. out of nowhere mike appeared by my side and helped me pry him off of this very bloody man and pinned him against the lockers but he was fighting us so hard it was honestly scaring me, i have never seen him like this before.

"Tyler come the fuck down!" Mike yelled at him trying to hold him against the lockers but its like tyler couldn't hear him.

"Tyler talk to me Bro." i said but again nothing he was full of rage and i don't know what to do.

"ENOUGH TY!" Jays voice all but ripped threw us, she didn't yell it but it was confident and stern. just like that tyler stopped fighting us and was now staring at jay and the fire slowly burned out, not all the way but enough for us to trust letting him go. Jay walked up to him and gave his hand a squeeze.

"Let's go the the gym, theres a better way to deal with all this. Come train with me and we will catch up with school this evening or tomorrow... and thank you Ty." she gave him a slight smile making him relax even more and he nodded his head. Then without saying anything they both walked out of here towards the school parking lot.

"Dude what the fuck!?" mike asked looking more shooken the i did at seeing his brother like that.

"I have no clue i had just got here. i have never seen him like that man, it honestly scared me." i admitted to mike who looked a bit scared himself.

"You? i have lived with him all my life, he is quiet and small but just now he was incontrollable and dangerous, i mean did you see that guy...so much blood." mike said then as a switch flipped we turned to were the guy who tyler was attacking was laying but he wasn't there anymore... just a pool of blood.

"Whered he go? i mean who was that guy?" mike asked as we looked up and down the halls.

"I don't know but when i got here he had jay pinned against the lockers and before i could do anything tyler was full on attack mode, i was to stunned to do anything at first." i said ignoring the shutters that traveled down my spine thinking of tylers raging face.

"Right he has gotten super protective over her, but still wont tell me what they talked about. Im not complaining just not use to him being so..." mike paused looking for the right word

"Confident" i said making him nod

"Right but im happy to know my little brother can handle his own" he chuckled making me laugh

"Handle his own? he almost killed that dude and we could barley hold him back...he is badass" i said and we laughed for a minute before deciding to let them have some time and we will catch up with them after school.

CHAPTER FIVE: TAG TEAM

JAY'S P.O.V.

"I'm sorry jay but when i heard what he said while he had you pinned against that locker i lost it. i couldn't stand seeing him pin you like that." Tyler say still a bit pissed about what happened. i thought back to earlier, after getting to school we all split up to our lockers and while i was at mine, Raider's slightly older brother showed up and pinned me against the lockers, i was exhausted and still in a lot of pain from last nights fight. Then he started calling me a slut and that i don't deserve his little brother, saying he was going to kill me before i go back with raider. i was starting to get scared then all of a sudden he was snatched off of me and tyler was on top of him in a second, he was hitting him so swiftly and hard that if Caiden and mike hadn't have stopped him then Raiders brother would have been dead.

"Don't be sorry, you protected me and i appreciate it but never do something so stupid again. This might have put you in raiders sights and that's not good ty." i told him not bothering sugar coating it.

"Jay you are my family and im going to protect you, you are just going to have to get use to that." he said stern and confident making it clear there is no use fighting. we remained silent throughout the ride and soon pulled into the gym. when we walked in X just looked at me then tyler quickly noticing his bloody fists but not saying anything as he continued signing up a new gym member. We walked to the back and i handed him some bandages and we wrapped our fists.

"I had a thought." i told tyler as we stood up and walked to the punching bags.

"Uh oh" he said as he started punching the bag while i held it.

"Though the situation wasn't great today i saw some real skills in you ty." i started making him stop punching and look at me with a stunned expression on his face

"Hear me out." i smiled at him " Your fast Ty and A lot stronger then you look which means components will underestimate you. You have been through a lot and this can be a good way to channel that. i would love to train you and help you focus this energy, i think you could become a unstoppable fighter ty." as i finished he was just look at me wide eyed.

"I don't know jay i have really done stuff like this." he said going back to punching

"Very true but that's what makes me believe you can become unstoppable, no training at all and you easily took down brad Raiders older brother. you got skills bro...lets put them to good use." i said and that made him smile big

"Alright let's do it." he said backing away from the back and walking towards the treadmill.

"Good, you run im going to talk to Xaiver." i told him unwrapping my fists and walking out of the room. I walked up to X who looked so bored at him desk.

"Hey X" i said giving him a side hug

"Wanna catch me up" he asked as i sat down

"As long as you don't over react." i stated knowing hes gonna get tense hearing that Raiders brother found me and that means he would tell marcus tho as far as i know raider never told Brad about marcus. He nodded but i knew better

I explained the events that went down today and as expected he was ready for me to move again

"X NO! When tyler attacked Brad to save me he put himself in the line of fire and if i run then they are left lone and will be targeted. im staying" i told him firmly and though he didn't like it he didn't argue.

"I think Tyler can become a damn good fighter, he's fast and stronger then he looks.
im going to train him." i stated and his angry turned to surprise.

"You don't train anyone, this is new." X said questiongly.

"He's my family now and i want to...he's got potential."i told him making him smile

"If you say he is then it's got to be true." he told me making me smile. I went back out to where Ty was and he was still running full speed on the tredmill.

"Hey good news i talked to X and we are going to get you a training membership here and you can train under me." i said to him as he stopped the tredmill and walked over to me.

"Great when do we start?" he asked excitedly.

"As much as i would like to start now i think you should talk to mike so he isn't blindsided by this? maybe Caiden too?" i told him because honestly i feel they should be apart of this part of his life.

"Will you help me explain it to them?" he asked getting nervous thinking about explaining it to them.
I nodded then looked at the clock on the wall and it was almost noon.

"Feel like heading back to school and getting free food?" i asked tyler who chuckled at me

"Yea let's do it." he said

CAIDEN'S P.O.V.

Mike and I were sitting in the cafeteria eating quietly at first when i noticed mike staring across the room, I look where he was staring right at Stacy his ex. She was popular but not the bitchy kind of popular, she was kind and always happy. Mike got messed up on night and cheated on her, she left him and he hasn't been the same since. He skip's from one girl to the other but i know he misses her, hell he loves her. i felt a frown on my face thinking about what he might be going through.

"You should just go talk to her bro." i told him making him snap his head towards me with a glare.

"Yea ill just walk right up to stacy and say what exactly? Hows lunch?" he snarked at me before shoving his plate away and laying his head that.

"Who's stacy?" i turned to see jay and tyler walking up to our table with a huge smile on jays face. mike shot up when he heard her.

"NOBODY!" mike yelled and instantly coward his head when the whole cafeteria silenced and all eyes were on him... including stacy's.

"Oh mind your own business." he glared at everyone but his eyes paused on stacy's softening then he looks at Jay.

"Yea nobody right" she laughed sitting down next to me and tyler sat next to mike. The table fell silent as my eyes and mikes fell on Tyler whos smile slowly faded.

"You two want to tell us what the hell went down this morning?" Mike asked looking over at jay then back at Tyler. Tyler nervously and almost pleadingly looked at Jay who smiled softly at him. "Okay" she whispered and he relaxed a little. She gave us the rundown on this Brad guy who i definitely don't like.

"I'm glad you were there Tyler." i told him because i would hate to think what would happen if he wasn't.

"Yea dude you were a beast, we could barley hold you back...my brother dominated his ass!" mike smiled from ear to ear wrapping an arm around Tyler's shoulder.

"About that..." Tyler started making us look at him a bit confused. Tyler looked over at Jay who gave a small nod then he continued.

"Jay and I have been talking and She wants to train me, and maybe even make me a fighter..." Tyler kind of spat it all out at ounce but i didn't miss how quick Mike's smile fell.

"Your kidding right?" He asked his brother but already knowing the answer by the look on his face

"I don't know about this tyler." Mike said shaking his head. Tyler looked at Jay with once again pleading eyes that made her sigh.

"Mike i know you have always been the tough one, the one who took all the crap so he wouldn't have to but you saw him this morning. Mike, Tyler has some serious skills and power and i saw all that from that one fight this morning. I know with some training and guidance ty can do some serious damage and all that pent up energy cant stay built up inside him but we wont go through with this if you don't want us to." Jay talked calmly and steady with her words and i just watched as mike analyzed every single one of them, to say he is protective is an understatement.

"I guess if this is what you really want Tyler, then im behind you completely." mike finally said after a moment of silence. i couldn't help but smile when mike said this i know it made tyler happy. The bell rang signaling lunch is over and we all stood to leave.

"Well i think im going to jet outta here, hell i aint been here all day anyways i just came for the free food today." Jay chuckled as she said this standing and grabbing her bag.

"Your not going to class?" i asked her in confusion

"nah its free period then Chemistry so ill just make it up tomorrow, i wanna get home and train a bit." she said with a shrug.

"Do you ever focus on anything besides training? Besides what about collage?" i asked her as we all walked down the halls.

"Nope i train so hard to remain undefeated and im not going to collage." when she said that i came to a full stop.

"Why not?" i asked her not understanding why she wouldn't want to further her education.

"No point, my fighting skills makes all the money i need." she replyed once again shrugging her shoulders.

"You don't want to fight forever do you?" i asked taking a step closer cupping her check with my hand. She seemed confused by my question and she was thinking on it rather hard.

"I can't imagine doing anything else, it's who i am...im a fighter a survivor." she said back almost whispering. i decided not to push my luck with her and take it slow so i let my hand fall from her face and stepped back to give her some space.

"Good enough for me." i told her making her smile and my stomach knots up yet again.

Damn that smile...

JAY'S P.O.V.

THREE WEEKS LATER...

"AGAIN!" I yell and tyler jabs left right right left kick. "Again" and he does as told.
We have been training for three weeks now and i got to say I knew tyler was good but he has progressed so fast it honestly had me super proud of him.

"Dang bro i would hate to get on you bad side." Caiden says holding out a water bottle for me.

"Thanks" i smile at him as i take it.

"I think i could take him." mike said walking up to tyler.

"Let's test that shall we?" i said motioning to the mat, tyler smirked and walked to the mat.

"Bring it bro." Ty said to mike as mike stepped onto the mat.

"Lets make this fun, underground rules... Black out or tap out." i said winking at tyler because i knew he had this in the bag. mike nodded and smirked as they got ready in opposite corners.

"You both ready?" X asked walking up to the mat interested to see how good tyler honestly is. both boys nods and he smiled.

"ok then, Ready steady fight!" X shouted and no sooner then he did tyler lunged for mike with quick and dangerous blows to mike. Left right left left right, he just keeps going then pins mike to the floor and just like that mike was tapping on the matt and tyler jumped off of him. i look over at X and his eyebrows were raised in surprise.

"Damn" i heard Caiden whisper and i couldn't stop smiling. Tyler walked up to me and gave me a sweaty hug.

"Eww bro you stink!" i fake gaged making him laugh as he walked over to mike who was still on the matt. he reached out his hand and helped mike up slowly.

"i thought you could take me bro?" Tyler asked earning a glare from mike and a laugh from me, Caiden, and Xaiver.

"Seems jay trained him better then i thought." mike said against gritted teeth.

"Maybe she should train you too." Xaiver said to him

"Yea bro we could fight together." tyler said getting a bit excited. Mike shook his head

"No dude this is your thing imma let you have it, football's my thing." Mike chuckled as he sat down holding his abdomine. Tyler started to frown a little but stopped when he saw me smirking.

"What?" he asked looking at me with furrowed eyebrows.

"I got ahold of Raider and set the fight up to be a tag team fight, i was thinking you'd like to be my partner for the fight?" i asked him smirking his eyes were wide as he looked at me.

"Really!?" he asked grinning wide, i shook my head at him.

"Wasn't training you for the hell of it, you got potential dude i'd be honored to have you fight with me." i said and he ran up to me giving me another sweaty hug.

"Yea yea now go hit the showers." i smiled at him making him chuckle and throw his hands up in surrender.

CHAPTER SIX: LET'S FIGHT

JAY'S P.O.V.

RED! That's what I saw right this minute as I swung the doors to the school open, I could feel the rage fuming off of me and student's made a path as I looked for my prey. I rounded the corner and spotted him.

"MIKE!" I roared as I made my way to him and him instantly jumped behind Caiden and Tyler trying to put distance between us, fear covering his face.

"Hand. him. over. now." I kept my death glare on Mike as if tyler and Caiden wasn't blocking most my view of him and my tone was calm but deadly.

"Woah calm down, what happened angel?" Caiden said trying to smirk but there was a hint of fear in his eyes.

"This is between me and the dead man cowering behind you two." I said gritting my teeth together.

"Sorry sis as much as I love you and respect you I cant hand him over unless I know what he has done." Tyler said chuckling and crossing his arms infront of his chest. For the first time since I found mike I snapped my gaze away from him sending tyler a stern glare before sending one to Caiden for calling me angle but even though my glare made them tense and even back up a little they didn't move.

"That fucker scratched my Baby...His ass is mine!" I spat jumping between them trying to get my hands on mike but failed miserably as the boys grabbed me and put me back infront of them.

"Its was an accident I swear jay!!" Mike pleaded with me looking terrified at this moment.

"I will not harm you because you are family but mark my words mike, there WILL be payback." I gave him a small evil smirk making him look even more afraid then before.

"I think id rather take the beating actually." Mike said coming out from behind them finally, making me smile even bigger.

"Nope, I think I already got a plan brewing now that i think about it." I smirked as I saw Meg and Danny heading our way.

"What did we miss?" Meg asked looking at Mike who hasn't taken his eyes off me looking horrified.

"Mikes a dead man...Scratched her car by accident." Caiden smirked and Danny's eyes went huge and Meg covered her mouth as a small gasp escaped, yes we all have gotten close these last few weeks and though meg and danny don't know of my fighting lifestyle or my background they do know how much I adore my car.

"I was just starting to like him too." Danny said slinging his arm over Megs shoulder making her blush.

"Hey meg I had a thought." I said smirking as my eyes are locked on Mikes wide eyes. I didn't think he could get any paler but he just did. I looked at meg who was smiling and nodding her head knowing it was going to be good.

"Say no more, no clue what it is but im in." She smiled brightly looking at mikes scared face.

"Im so dead." Mike mumbled looking down at the ground shaking his head. The bell rang and we all headed to Gym Except Meg, she had a different class this period, but danny walked her to her class.

"You know your hot when your mad." I hear Caiden whisper in my ear and felt his hot breath on my neck sparking a burning fire deep inside of me. I didn't turn to look at him because he was standing to close, close enough I could smell his cologne and it made my head fuzzy. I smirked then jerked my elbow back making contact with his abdomen and he stubled and slumped over holding his stomach gasping for air.

"Opps im so sorry you startled me." I said with fake worry all over my face but I couldn't help but let a smirk settle on my lips. I looked over to see Mike and tyler laughing as they walked towards us from the changing rooms.

"Yea...Right..." Was all Caiden could say as he try's to stand up straight.
Just as Tyler and mike get's to us Danny comes into the gyms smiling from ear to ear as he walks up to us.

"So guess what?" He said as he got up to us looking extremely happy.

"You and meg finally going out?" I asked making everyone smirk and look at Danny who was now Red as a tomato.

"What! NO! we are best friends that it!" Danny stuttered out not making any eye contact at all.

"Uh huh whatever you say" I said smirking at him

"What is it then?" Tyler asked as he slung his arm over my shoulder and I leaned my head on his shoulder waiting for Danny to answer.
this had become a regular thing with me and tyler, we have become extremely close even closer then I ever was with jake. Now that Ty has started training he has gained muscle and eyes of a lot of girls in this school which means more glares at me, they don't know he's gay and I think he likes the confidence boosts so we keep it that way.

"I got a Job!" Danny beamed at us ignoring the comment I made.

"Sweet Bro where at." Caiden asked giving him a fist bump.

"Um..im Sorta gonna be the new D.J at the Arch a new club in town."
He said smirking and rubbing the back of his neck

"That's awesome dude when do you start?" I asked leaving tylers arms
and giving danny a big hug.

"First night is tonight, can you guys come? Meg will be there." Danny
asked looking at all of us. Everyone nodded except me I just looked
at him as all eyes fell on me.

"Please?" He asked with puppy dog eyes and I rolled my eyes but
couldn't help but smile.

"Fine but you have to come to my party this Saturday." I smirked
at him as everyone shouted in unison

"WHAT?"

I couldn't help but laugh

"You hate parties." Tyler stated looking at me questioningly

"Let alone you never throw them." Caiden added in quirking his
eyebrows

"Yea well I am this Saturday and you all have to be there." I
stated matter-of-factly

"ok I gotta see this" mike said smiling and I bit down the smirk
that wanted to form on my face... oh if you only knew what I

had planned you would never show up.

CAIDEN'S P.O.V.

It was about seven at night and the guys and I were all in the living room of their house waiting for jay to finish getting ready for the club. We all have gotten close over the past few week's and Jay finally opened up a little bit to us. She told us that she had an older brother named Jake and they use to be close but he betrayed her, that sick bastard let his father beat her and use her for fights. She told us all about Raider and to expect him to make a scene if he looses.

The room went silent and everyone was looking at the stairs, I turned to look and lost my breath. Jay Was wearing a tight fitted Bright red dressed that hugged her in all the right ways. Her hair was curled and she had a light layer of make up on and I know tonight is going to be the death of me.

"What do you think? I don't really dress up much?" She asked walking over to us.

"Shit..." Mike said eyes glued to her and Tyler smaked him upside the head then nodded over at me. I saw mike shrug out the corner of my eyes but I couldn't stop looking at Jay. she walked up to me and smiled

"So?" she eyes with a bright spark in her eyes

"Wow" Was all I was able to say but it was enough to make her blush and I smiled

"You look hot can we go now?" Danny said breaking our eye contact I sent him a glare for interrupting my moment.
Jay chuckled and nodded walking towards the door.

"asshole." I muttered under my breath as I followed them out making tyler and mike chuckle. We followed jay to the club, Meg and Tyler rode with her and mike and danny road with me. It's nothing new Tyler and her are always together and I honestly don't mind. I think mikes only riding with me because he is still scared of Jay's payback. We pulled up to the club and parked next to Jay. we all walked up to the club which was pretty packed and I didn't miss all the animal like looks jay got from people whether it was threatened females or hungry looking men and I did not like it one bit. Once we got in Danny disappeared to get set up and meg went with him. Mike was already talking to some Red head on the dance floor and I couldn't help but shake my head...Man whore. Jay, Tyler, Rafal, and I found a table and took our seats, I slid in next to my girl and tyler sat next to Rafal.

"SO HOWS TRAINING BEEN?" Rafal shouted above the music

and crowd so jay and tyler could hear him.

"REALLY GOOD. I THINK HES READY FOR HIS FIRST FIGHT." Jay replied looking at a now smiling tyler. Rafal wrapped his arm around Ty and smiled wide.

"DAMN RIGHT HE IS, HES A NATURAL." Rafal said beaming with pride. I got to say I love how happy they are.

"Imma go get something to drink you guys want anything?" Jay said standing up.

"Nah im good." I said smiling at her. I didn't want to drink in case anyone tries something with her... I mean because im driving home

"i'll come with you." Rafal said standing up.

"Surprise me babe." Tyler said winking at rafal. I watched as they walked to they bar to order their drinks and I couldn't take my eyes off of her. She was laughing at something Rafal said and her hair swayed when she did, this women was absolutely Brilliant.

"Dude when are you going to tell her how you feel?" I heard tyler asked making me snap my gaze to him.

"When its the right time." I stated not questioning how he knows, and I definitely don't lie to my boys.

"When will it ever be?" He asked giving me a pointed look. I ignored that look and glanced back over at my Angel.

"When she's ready." I said and when I looked back at tyler who was smiling brightly obviously liking my answer with his over protective self.

"Well brother I suggest you make it the right time before someone else does." He stated nodding his head in jays direction and I instantly looked over to see some man in jeans and a black tee shirt with tatts all down his arm. he tapped her arm and she turned to look at him then glanced at me before returning her gaze to that asshole. I felt fire burn inside of me when I saw her smile at something he said. She said something to him then pointed at me smirking as our gaze locked. The man threw his hands up in surrender then walked away, before they headed back to the table.

"What was that about?" I asked her as she sat next to me.

"Some guy wanting to dance, told him I was with my boyfriend but he didn't believe me." she shrugged and I felt the smile form on my face

"And you said I was your boyfriend huh Angel?" I asked winking at her

"well you were looking at him mighty pissed so I figured it would line up." she smirked before taking a sip of her drink

We spent the rest of the night talking and dancing at some point mike finally showed up half drunk with a hickey on his neck. I have to admit Danny was pretty good At DJing and the crowd definitely loves him. After jay got hit on I pretty much didn't leave her side for the night

After we got back to Jay's Rafal took a very drunk Tyler to his room and Jay helped me get Mike to his bedroom.

"They are going to feel like shit in the morning." She snickered as we walked out of mikes room and towards her room.

"I think imma get some laps in before bed, your welcome to stay if you want." she smiled at me before going into her room and changing. I decided to wait by the pool for her to come out and even though I have seen her in a bikini before im still sitting here drooling like an idiot when she gets out here.

"Have mercy.." I whispered but I think she heard it because she blushed and started smirking.

JAY'S P.O.V.

I finish up my laps and as I climb out Caiden hands me a towel. I look up at him and smile as I grab it.

"Thank you." I said. he watched me for the past hour just swimming back and forth, it was honestly sweet but a tad unsettling because I can't tell what he's thinking.

"You looked absolutely stunning tonight jay." he said taking a step closer and I locked my eyes on his beautiful ocean filled eyes as he reached up and pushed a strand of wet hair behind my ear. I swallowed hard unable to move even a inch.

"Jay..." he pretty much whispered as he towered over me and the butterflies In my stomach stopped me from speaking. "Can I kiss you?" he whispered and all caution went out the window, just for tonight, just this once... I needed to do this. I didn't respond instead I grabbed his waist and stood on my tip toes as I lightly pressed my lips against his. He tensed obviously shocked that I kissed him instead of pulling away like I have been but I have been holding back for a minute and it is driving me insane I needed to do this. The kiss turned from slow to heated as I opened my mouth to allow him entrance when he slides his tongue against my bottom lip. After a minute of heavy kissing all my senses hit me like a train and I pulled away and rested my forehead on his.

"We can't.." I said trying to catch my breath

"I know." he said catching me by surprise making me look at him, does he though. The nightmares haven't gotten any better, im still seeing him get shot by marcus over and over and I don't want him getting that involved with marcus if I can help it.

"Your not ready, but I want you to know im here angel...Always going to be here." he said before placing a kiss on my forhead and making butterflies erupt in my stomach. these past few weeks I have gotten close to these boys but things with Caiden are different. He terrifies me, I can't see myself surviving him getting hurt because of me. I am not sure what im feeling for him but I know that I wont be able to avoid these feelings forever, but hopefully long enough to figure them out.

"I should get home, but ill see you guys tomorrow." he smiled at me and I nodded and walked him to the front door. after he left I went to shower then headed to bed. My sleep has been even worse then usual, ill be lucky to get four or five hours of sleep now thanks to the nightmares involving Caiden.

I woke up around four sweaty and panting then did my usual, eat, practice, shower. Before I knew it the boys were coming into the kitchen and though mike looked perfectly normal, Tyler looked like he was the walking dead. I handed him a cup of juice and some advil. He gave a weak smile before taking the medicine and laying hi head on my shoulder.

"Never let me drink again." he mumbled quietly probably with a pounding headache

"Awe babe im sorry, I promise no more." I said rubbing his back but grinning knowing last night he was going to regret that fifth shot.

"Come on yall lets get to school! whooh!!" Mike yelled as her claps his hands next to Tylers Head making him jump and glare at his brother.

"Asshole." Tyler mumbled before turning and laying his head back on my shoulder.

"Do I have to go today?" He asked giving his best sad voice.

"Yes its pizza Friday, but ill let you outta training tonight." I said making him sit up and slowly making our way towards the door.

"Fiiinnneee" He groaned stomping towards the car making mike and I Chuckle at his poutyness. As we got to School Caiden was already there sitting on his car waiting on us to get here. I parked next to him and we all got out and headed towards the building, Tyler slung his arm over my shoulder as we entered the school.
The day went on as usual, ignoring Beths glares and the butterflies Caiden gives me everytime I look at him and catch him already staring at me.

We are sitting in the lunchroom talking about how messed up The guy's got last night went my phone started ringing, I looked down and it was Xaiver.

"Sup?" I answered and the table went silent as all

eyes fell on me.

"Hey you got a second?" X asked on the other end of the line

"shoot." I replied

"How's tylers training going?" He asked making me get up from the table and walk a couple feet away so Meg and Danny don't hear.

"He's progressed really good, I think he's almost ready for his first fight." I told him as I twirled my hair around my fingers.

"Good to hear because I have a fight lined up for him, sunday night." X more said then asked.

"Sounds good ill let him know." I said hanging up and nodding for the guys to meet me in the hallways away from meg and danny. when they got out there I turned to face them with a smile on my face as I locked eyes with Tyler.

"X called, said he has a fight for you if you want it." I told him.

"You think your ready?" Mike asked looking at his brother who just smirked then looked at me.

"Let's fight." He said with a glint in his eyes.

CHAPTER SEVEN: SURPRISE

JAY'S P.O.V.

"Ok, we are alone so spill, whats your genius plan for revenge?" Meg Grinned as she sat on my bed hugging a pillow. I walked over and sat next to her smiling as I faced her.

"So you know his story with his ex right?" I asked grinning ear to ear as she gasped and covered her mouth.

" I'll take that as a yes." I smiled at her as I continued

"So Mike has been avoiding any parties or places she shows up at because as guilty as he feels for that mistake ,and trust me he feels guilty, he cant keep his eyes off of her." I paused making sure shes with me and she nods for me to continue.

" Anyways it isn't any secret he regrets his decision and is constantly wishing he could take this back, well as payback she's going to be at the party tonight." I told Meg and her eyes went wide

"WHAT!!" she yelled and I actually had to cover my ears

"Shhh" I hushed her putting a finger to my lips.

"Don't you think that's kinda mean tho?" She asked looking guilty

"Under normal circumstances yes but he will only be feeling

the revenge part of the night for a few minutes before something hopefully good happens." I said look at a very confused looking meg.

"How can anything good happen with this? and how do you know she is going to come?" meg asked

"I talked to her earlier and explained how mike is and feels, and she already knew by the way he watched her and acted when shes around, she said she noticed that he will never let his gaze settle on any other women when she is in the same room. She also said that she misses him so shes gonna surprise show up at the party and im gonna make sure he has no choice but to talk to her...that's where the new cheerleader Amber comes in, so heres what we do..." I watched her reaction as I told her the plan and her smile only grew on her face.

â€¦PARTY TIME...

We are all standing around the house I had rented for the party, yes I rented a house for the party because one I didn't want a bunch of idiots drunk and messing up my home and also because I didn't need a lot of people knowing where I live at because im still laying low, and the plan will be set in motion hopefully soon. I watch as Mike and one of his football buddies argue back and forth over the music about who was the most valued player and I see Caiden watching me again, I turned and looked at him offering him a small smile which he returned but didn't take his eyes off of me and I couldn't help but blush and look back at mike so Caiden didn't see my red face.

"I can't believe it I mean im here and still can NOT believe you threw this bomb ass party!" Mike said looking over at me smiling.

"Oh the nights young and the party has just started love." I said sending him a wink which he smirked at while returning one.
The tall football buddy of Mikes took this as an opportunity to introduce himself to me.

"Im Zach I don't think we have been introduced."he said as he took my hand and kissed it but I didn't miss the cocky smirk he had on his face while he did so, idiot. I saw meg around the corner and she gave me a thumbs up, I pulled my hand out of zachs and gave him a small smile.

"Cool I will be back in a few guys." I said walking past them and up the stairs to where meg is waiting for me.

"Is it time?" I asked her

"Yes, stacy is all set up where you said and I just talked to amber and she is ready." she said and we both surpressed a laugh.

"Ok showtime." I said and we headed back down stairs so nobody came looking.

"Where'd you go?" Caiden asked as I got back over there, I just shrugged my shoulders and ignored his question. Tyler came out of nowhere and slung his arm over my shoulder, He wasn't in on the plan since he has been with Rafal all day I hadn't really filled him in.

"What did I miss?" He asked as he grabbed my Monster and drank some. Just then Amber walks in and right up to mike with her best seductive look. Right on time.
I watched as she wrapped her hand around his arm and started whispering in his ear and I had to surpress a smile when I saw him grinning. She then nodded to the Stairs and he sent her a wink before looking over at us.

"If you will excuse me, ill be right back." Mike said sending me a cheeky grin.

I slowly followed behind them but stayed close enough so I could grab him when we get up there. We got to the top of the stairs and just as they were about to walk into a bedroom Amber pulled away taking quick steps back and I grabbed ahold of him before he could register what was happening and with all my strength I shoved him into the room...He did indeed loose his footing and stumble to the floor face first..oof. I wip out my phone and turn on the camera ready for this picture.

"WHAT THE HELL JAY!!!" He roared as he started to get up and his eyes were locked on me as he stood.

" WHAT WAS THAT!?!?" He yelled and started to take a step forward when he noticed the camera and movement out of the corner of his eyes. He snapped his head and I snapped the picture...All color left his face and his eyes buldged out of his head while his jaw hung open. I noticed that he was even shaking a little.

"Stacy?" he mumbled her name like he couldn't believe it was her.
I took this moment to exit knowing I got my revenge but now it's time they work this shit out alone. As I closed the door I came face to face with Everyone and when I say everyone I mean Tyler, Caiden, Rafal, Danny, Meg, and Amber. The girls had excited looks while the guys look confused and I finally let out a laugh and nodded for them to follow me.

When we got outside I turned and faced them then caught the guys up on our plan before showing them the picture of Mikes face when he saw stacy. They were on the ground laughing after seeing the picture and I about joined them...it was awesome.

"Oh...my...god..." Tyler laughed and said in-between breaths still clutching his stomach.

"Remind me never to piss you off." Caiden smiled at me as he wiped a tear from his face that fell from laughing so hard. After a couple more minutes everyone had finished laughing and we walked back inside and towards the kitchen to wait for Mike.

"Hey good looking, you know I still haven't caught your name." Zach said walking into the the kitchen and straight up to me I rolled my eyes and just took a sip of my drink hopeing he would take this hint since he missed the last one.

"Come on im not asking for much now am I?" Zach pushed and took another step towards me.

"Back off Zach she isn't interested" Caiden said a step closer to us now standing right beside me glareing at Zach.

"Oh my bad bro I didn't realize someone had already claimed that ass." Zach smirked sending a wink to me which made me look at him in disgust.

"Fuck off prick." Tyler spat coming up on my left and swinging an arm around my shoulder keeping a hard glre on Zach.

"Oh you guys are sharing her then, well then you shouldn't care if I take a turn." He smirked at tyler and I had about had enough of his mouth. Tyler started to go for Zach but I caught his arm and pulled him back. I took two steps twards Zach and smirked.

"See she's down." Zach winked at me and I drew back and delivered a right hook making him stumble to the left . he touched his face and saw blood then looked at me with heat in his eyes...

"Fucking Bitch!" He yelled and just as he was about to swing at me and before I could beat the shit out of him an Angry voice rang through the house making everyone go silent.

"WHAT THE FUCK ARE YOU DOING ZACH!!!" Mikes angry voice rang through the house and Zach spun around to come face to face with a pissed mike.

"Little bitch hit me" Zach spat the blood on the ground and I smirked.

"You deserved it too." Caiden piped in making me chuckle.
Zach snapped his eyes at me and reached towards me but was slammed against the wall by mike.

"Fucking touch her and I will end you Anderson!" Mike spat at him as venom traced his words.

"You look at her...touch her...or talk about her and your ass is mine!" Mike spat before slamming him against the wall hard then walking over to me.

"Mind if stacy comes back with us for a bit tonight?" He asked smiling at me, I gave him a wicked smirk then nodded.

"Yea I hate parties anyhow let's get outta here." I chuckled and walked towards the door while the rest followed laughing behind me.

CAIDEN'S P.O.V.

"I swear to god jay you better not even think about posting that!" Mike glared at jay as she showed him the picture of him when he saw stacy at the party but she just smirked as she slid her phone into her back pocket and shrugged.

"Better be extra nice lover boy." She smirked at him as stacy giggled at what she said. We were all Back at Jay's place sitting in the living room trying to give mike hell about the look on his face in the photo. Mike and stacy sat cuddled up on one couch while tyler was sprawled out on the floor, Rafal had headed home about an hour ago as did Meg and Danny, Jay and I were sitting on the second couch laughing at a very red stacy.

"Well all in all it was a great revenge and a kind thing for you to do, so thank you Jay." Stacy smiled at her and jay just nodded.

"Hey you mind if I crash here tonight?" I asked jay making her look up at me with those bright green eyes swimming with golden fire and I ached to stare into those eyes for as long as she would allow me too.

"You know you don't need to ask, you'll always have a room here when you need it." She smiled at me but not looking away. I smiled at her as she quickly realized we were staring at each other and she looked away but I did not miss that blush. She quickly cleared her throat and stood up.

"Well I think I am going to get some sleep it's getting late, Ty you have training tomorrow so I suggest you do the same." She said as she headed to the stairs. "Fine" Tyler replied but stuck out his tongue since her back was turned to him.

"I saw that" She yelled as she went up the stairs making me smirk as tylers eyes widened.

"Great shes gonna train me even worse now tomorrow." He mumbled as he stomped up the stairs and to his room making me chuckle.

"Alright love birds im going to bed so try to keep it down tonight." I said earning a smirk from mike.

"No promises." he said making Stacy turn bright red as she slapped his arm.

"Oh no we have so much more to talk about before that happens mister." She gave him a glare and I chuckled as I headed up the stairs when I heard mike say something about talking with their bodies earning him a loud slap from stacy. I paused infront of Jay's door and saw the light was off but I knew she couldn't have fallen asleep that quick but I decided to let her try and rest.
I went to the room down the hall and crawled into the extremely

comfortable bed making me realize how tired I actually was, soon everything went hazy and I was drifting off to sleep.

I woke up really thirsty and checked the time on my phone, I had to blink a couple times and rub my eyes before my vision cleared up and it was almost four in the morning. I got out of bed and crept downstairs not wanting to wake anyone up. After drinking a couple small glasses of water I headed back up stairs and to my room, I was in my room and about to close the door when I heard the faint sound of a door closing making me turn towards the hall. I waited and didn't hear anything but a few seconds later Jay came walking past my room but she didn't notice my door open or me standing there, she was really zoned out. I peered into the hall and watched as she walked into the gym and I followed her taking in her appearance, ignoring the tight leggings and sports bra I noticed she was pale and when I opened the gym door my heart sank. Jay was sitting on the bench wrapping her knuckles still unaware of my presence but what worried me was the fact that she was soaking wet from head to toe and shaking before doing any training. I slowly walked up to her and bent down.

"Angle..." I whispered making her jump and snap her eyes up to mine, she had been crying and her eyes were red and puffy.

She didn't say anything but the water kept building in her eyes.

"Angle what is it?" I asked again only in a whisper as I put my hand on her arm and slowly rub circles with my thumb. She still didn't speak just swallowed hard. " Did you have a nightmare?" I asked her and she didn't answer at first but then slowly nodded her head yes and a couple tears escaped her eyes and ran down her cheek.

"do you want to talk about it?" I ask her and she shakes her head no quickly not giving herself time to even think about the answer.

"Ok that's fine but its a big day and Tyler is going to need you alert and not exhausted why don't you try to lay back down?" I ask hoping tyler will be enough to motivate her to rest, I don't like it when she run's herself like this, its not healthy not with what she does for a living. she nods her head and sets her bandages down. I stand and hold out my hand and she takes it without speaking and slowly stands up. I lead her out of the gym and towards her room but she stop Halfway down the hall, I turn and look at her and shes looking at the floor.

"What is it?" I ask walking up to her placing my finger under her chin making her look up at me gently.

"I ..I don't want to be alone tonight...Can I please stay with you just this once?" she asked as another tear ran down her cheek. I leaned in and kissed her forehead before pulling her into a hug.

"You know you don't have to ask, you always be welcome to stay with me when you are scared or just don't want to be alone." I said mimicking what she told me earlier. she chuckled and pulled away.

"Sounds a little familiar." She said with a smile that melted my world. I smiled and led her into the room I was staying in and I crawled into the bed, She lays down right next to me and I wrap my arm around her waist and pulled her into me nuzzling my nose into the crook of her neck. I felt her breathing even out and noticed she was quickly asleep and I couldn't help but to smile, she wanted to stay with me tonight and that meant everything to me. I fell asleep with a smile on my face knowing right then and there that my life will never be the same after knowing Jay Moore...

She has stole my heart and I never want it back.

JAY'S P.O.V.

As I opened my eyes I couldn't help but smile when I stretched,

I had actually got some rest last night. I went back to sleep and didn't continue my nightmare. It feels good I honestly don't remember the last time I got some rest, wait I shared a bed with Caiden. At that thought I shot up and scanned the bed and room but Caiden wasn't there and before I knew it a frown had formed on my lips but I shook it off, I need to get ready.

After a quick shower I got dressed and packed my training gear, I looked at the time and it was 6:30 in the morning and I couldn't help but smile again thinking of how much rest I actually got. As I got down stairs I was both proud and stunned at what I saw. I was proud to see Tyler up and with all his gear packed and waiting by the front door while he was eating breakfast but what shocked me was Caiden was downstairs wearing workout clothes and was drinking a protein shake, I thought he would be gone by now.

"Morning boys." I saw walking into the kitchen.

"Hey" They both said looking up to me when I walked in, I lock eyes with Caiden and he gives me a soft smile and I return the gesture, im not ready for the questions yet.

"Glad to see your up and ready on time." I smirked at tyler as he glares at me.

"That's because I have my first fight tonight." He says as his eyes narrow and my smirk only widens

"Oh really? I thought it had something to do with the last time I had to wake you up you got covered in half melted ice." I said and Caiden busted out laughing "WHAT!!" he yelled

"Your evil." Tyler glared at me before shoving more food into his mouth and I couldn't help but laugh.

"She's awesome." Caiden said making me look over at him and he is staring at me in a way that makes my heart pound in my chest. I smile at him and mouth a silent thank you in which he winks at me making me blush and look away.

"Well are you about ready to start training?" I asked tyler ignoring the heat rising in my abdomen from the intense gaze Caiden has on me. Tyler nods and stands up taking his plate to the kitchen

"Mind training one more?" Caiden asks standing from the table making me snap my eyes to him and give him a questioning look.

"Explain?" I said with a quirked eyebrow and he just smirked and shrugged his shoulders.

"I don't want to be a fighter by no means but I would like to have your back if or when the time comes." He said and I couldn't help but smile.

"Better be able to keep up." I winked at him and this time it was him that blushed and shook his head.

"Lets start with the gym, grab ur stuff and meet me in there in about five minutes Ty. Caiden i'll get you set up with some of the stuff your going to need for training, follow me." I said and headed towards the gym room. I walked straight to the shelf at the back of the room and started shuffling threw the stuff,

Bandages...check
Tape...check
Wraps...check
Rags...check
Backpack...check
Water bottle...check
First aid kit...Check

As I was going through the checklist in my head and piling stuff in my arms I didn't even hear The door close nor did I hear Caiden walk up and stand right behind me. I felt his warm hands lightly grab both sides of my waist and he gently but swiftly pulls me against him so my back is touching his chest and I couldn't help the gasp that left my lips. I felt him lean in and I could feel his warm breath hitting my ear making me reactively flutter my eyes closed unable to breath or think, his voice was a low whisper but was deep and sent shivers down my spine "How did you sleep angel?" he asked

"Im..uh I slept better then I have in years after I went back to sleep." I managed to stutter out but only really focusing on the sparks radiating from his touch and from his breath.

"Turn around angel." He said and I felt his arms drop and no longer could feel his breath on my neck telling me he backed up. I took a deep breath trying to compose myself and I slowly turned around but couldn't face him instead I stared at the stuff in my arms.

"you gonna put that stuff down or is it that fun to look at?" he chuckled making me roll my eyes but refuse to let him see the smile I was suppressing while i sat the stuff on the bench next to me. I looked him in the eyes as he walked up to me and grabbed my hand.

"Can I ask you something?" he said not in a whisper but still a low tone. I nodded not trusting my voice right this second.

"What did you mean when you said it was the best sleep in years?" he asked and I honestly wasn't expecting it and really didn't realize I even said that, damn the effect he has on me.

"Um I don't really sleep more then four maybe five hours tops a night and that's if im lucky." I told him unable to tear away from his eyes, like im entranced. he furrowed his eyebrows together "You can't be serious?" he asked trying to see if im joking. I was able to tear my eyes off him at this moment and took a deep breath stepping away and sitting down.

" I have nightmares, I can't talk about them but it was mostly just memories so when I have them I usually train so I don't have to think or go back to sleep but last night I was able to rest...without nightmares...because of you." I all but mumbled the last part, he took a step towards me and was about to say something when Tyler came in.

"Alright lets train." he said not realizing what was going on and man was I happy to end this conversation...

Saved by the bell.

CHAPTER EIGHT: OH BROTHER

JAY'S P.O.V.

"Are you sure your ready" Mike asked Tyler who was running in place trying to calm his anxiety but he wont admit it.

"Im beyond ready, right Jay?" Tyler said as he smirked and looked over at me but I could tell he really needed to hear me say it.

"You are by far my prize puple...the other guy wont know what hit him Ty" I said grinning wide and I adored how his eyes lit up when I said it.

"Hey! what about me?" Caiden said from beside me faking a hurt expression making me roll my eyes and chuckle.

"You sir just started training and have a ways to go." I sent him a smirk when I said that but it wasn't all that true, Caiden has some good skills himself but I don't really want him in the ring it just didn't feel right and definitely wasn't safe for him. He gave me a fake glare and I shook my head smiling. I seem to be smiling a lot lately with these guys and I don't hate it either.

"Jay you should finish getting your mask and paint on, Tyler is on soon" X said poking his head out his office door but retreating before I have time to say anything. I sigh and walk over to the mirror and sit down. While I applied the paint and mask I noticed Caiden's intense gaze on my back, I glance at him in the mirror and our eyes lock. I give him a small smile and he returns one. Breaking eye contact I stand and throw on my jacket, giving myself a once over once I was satisficed I turned and looked at tyler who was now sitting down.

"Ready Beast?" I asked tyler with a smile and he grinned back at me. We decided on Beast to be his fighting name because in beauty and the beast when the beast goes from man to well, beast and when you see tyler all you see is some small guy but when its time to fight the beast in him comes out and I know he will win.

"Lets do this." tyler said giving his brother and Caiden a fist bump.

"Good luck bro." mike said as him and Caiden walk out to get ready to watch the fight. I walked out of the private dressing room with tyler slightly behind me on my right and Xaiver appeared on my left right next to him. we walked silently and stopped right behind the big curtain, I turned to look at Ty.

"Alright as we talked about, i'll go out and announce you as my fighter when I draw out your name that's your cue, got it?" I asked him and he nodded taking a deep breath.

"You got this." X said to him patting him on the back

"No Doubt" I smiled and walked threw the curtain and the crowd went from loud to Crazy, they knew who I was by the paint and jacket. I kept my face blank as I walk to the center with X right behind me, we got in the ring and he handed me the microphone.

"ALRIGHT ALRIGHT ALRIGHT ALL YOU FIGHTER FANS SETTLE DOWN CAUSE I HAVE SOMETHING BIG TO SAY!" I roared above the crowd and like a switch was flipped they were silent and all eyes were on me, good.

"THAT'S BETTER. NOW THIS IS THE FIRST TIME YOU HAVE HEARD DIRECTLY FROM ME AND FOR THOSE WHO DONT KNOW ME I AM DEMON THE FUCKING CHAMPION AND TONIGHT YOU WILL BE MEETING A FIGHTER I HAVE, FOR THE FIRST TIME, TAKEN UNDER ME AND TRAINED HIM NOT THAT HE NEEDED MUCH, DUDES A NATURAL, SO ID LIKE YOU ALL TO GIVE A PROPER UNDERGROUND WELCOME TO THE NEWEST UP AND COMER... BEEEAAASSSTTT!!!" I roared his name and he didn't miss a beat, when he came threw the curtain the crowd did as told and screamed as loud as they could as he made his way to the ring. He climbed in the ring and met me in the middle, I passed the mic to X and locked hands with Ty as we brought our foreheads together resting against the others with our eyes closed and then pulled away and headed to the corner.

"FACING OUR CHAMPIONS FIRST AND ONLY FIGHTER, IS AN OLDIE BUT A GOODIE, COMING BACK AFTER LOOSING HIS TITLE IS BRUTE THE BRUTTTAAALLLL!!" X yelled into the microphone and I snapped my head to X who conveniently refused to make eye contact with me, asshole could have gave me a heads up. I looked at tyler who was looking nervous.

"Hey no! you got this Beast... stay focused, find his weak point, tune out the crowd." I locked eyes on his and he relaxed a little and started shaking his head, he looked over my shoulder and locked eyes on who I assume is brute. Xavier nodded for me to get out of the ring and I did so.

"SAME RULES AS ALWAYS BOYS, TAP OUT OR BLACK OUT!!!" x roared then walked out the ring and before I knew it the buzzer went off signaling the fighters to start. Tyler was to nervous because he didn't go at him as hard at first, he hesitated which landed him a hard right hook that he will feel later from brute. Ty recovered quickly and then I saw his usual fire he had during training and I grinned. He wasted no time and went at brute with hard jabs.

right, left, right, right, left, kick.

He was moving so pass I couldn't keep up let alone Brute, tyler finished with a solid uppercut making brute fall to the ground blacked out and blood everywhere. The crowd went deadly silent and then erupted in roars and claps, X got on stage and held his hand up and I adored it when Ty did the same thing I always do, give the crowd a hard blank stare and give them a small nod.

"AND OUR WINNER, DEMONS VERY OWN CHAMP, BEAAASSTTT!!!" X roared above the crowd and I took this time to climb into the ring, only then did tyler smile and when his eyes locked with mine. He met me halfway and we locked both our head and pressed our foreheads together like before the fight. We pulled apart and walked backstage, as soon as we got back the Tyler was attacked by mike and Caiden hugging him.

"Dude you were a literal beast!" Mike said hugging tyler

"Never doubted you bro" Caiden said fist bumping him then looked over at me "you have a damn good teacher."

I couldn't help but smile.

"Hell yeah I do." Tyler smirked and walked up to me hugging me tight.

"How was it?" I asked him pulling away from the hug to look up at him.

"Unlike anything I have ever felt before, I get why you do this now." Ty smiled at me brightly and I nodded to him

"Welcome to fight club" I smirked at him

CAIDEN'S P.O.V

That fight was badass I mean who knew tyler had it in him to take down brute, I was so proud of him. It was about six in the morning and I was sitting at the breakfast table with mom and may before school when I noticed my mom amd may staring at me.

"What?" I asked looking back and forth between the two.

"Well you been gone a lot lately..." my mom started and I knew where this was going.

"and you were just staring at your bacon smiling lost in Lalaland." she continued raising an eyebrow

"I like bacon" I glared at may playfully and took a bite of her bacon from her plate

"Hey!! I like bacon more!!!" may yelled at me and I chuckled

"Got to go, meeting the gang at school." I smirked as I got up and grabbed my stuff then put my leftover bacon on mays plate giving her a kiss. I walked over to mom and kissed her head and walked toward the front door, before I walked out I called out

"I will bring her over soon I promise." I chuckled as I walked out the door and heard them cheering and laughing, weirdos. As I got to school they were already out front waiting on me and I parked next to them and climbed out of my car, I instantly noticed the bruise on tylers eyes and smirked knowing he was proud of it. I looked at jay and my eyes lit up, she was wearing tight jeans and a red crop top with a black leather jacket and she looked hot as hell. her cheeks turned red telling me she noticed me checking her out and I smiled liking the effect I have on her.

The day went on as usual right up until lunch, we decided to eat outside because it was bright out and thankfully almost everyone was inside so we could sit outside in peace.

"Dude everyone lost their shit when you knocked brute out." Mike chuckled shoving some fries into his mouth.

"Taking after my mentor I guess." tyler smirked at jay and she smiled giving him a nod.
Jay's smile instantly dropped and for a minute I saw pure fear in her eyes that turned to extreme rage as her eyes locked on something over my shoulder. I wasn't the only one who noticed but before anyone could say anything she threw her tray off her lap and stormed past us. I turned to see a tall Man that had looked simular to jay but different in a lot of ways the look on his face went from sadness to fear as his eyes widened and he threw his hands up

"Wait wait wait" was all he said before she attacked

"YOU SON OF A BITCH!!" she screamed at him while pounding him over and over we rushed over to her and tyler was by her side in an instant with me and mike right behind him, she didn't even notice us screaming at her to calm down as we tired to pull her off, all three of us finally managed to get her a couple feet away from the now very bloody man as she screamed and kicked and tried to swing on him more

"ILL FUCKING KILL YOU DO YOU HEAR ME, YOU ARE DEAD!!" She screamed as she tried to get after him, the guy finally got to his feet and spit out some blood before speaking

"I promise little bird, ill never tell anyone your here...one day ill explain." was all he said before he took off and disappeared into the woods.

I grabbed jay who was still fighting to get to him but when I looked at her my heart broke, this was more then rage this was pain she was crying and shaking I just wrapped my arms around her and held her tight she stoped fighting me and started crying hard. I looked over at tyler and mike whos eyes were wide and they just stood there not sure what the hell just happened. After a few minutes she stopped crying and pulled away turning towards the woodline and just stared.

"Jay.." tyler whispered taking a step towards her.

"Jay who was that" He pushed when she didn't say anything. she slowly turned to look at us and we all instantly tensed up, her eyes were ice cold and her face hard. At that very moment we saw no pain or fear in her eyes we saw nothing but empty hate.

"Jake." She all but whispered his name but we all heard it, he fucking brother and we let him get away.

JAY'S P.O.V.

I couldn't be here right now, I needed to get out of there and I did not wait for them to say anything before I turned and walked to my car. As I was walking away I heard Caiden and mike calling for me but I couldn't talk right now then I heard tyler faintly but sternly tell them to give me some space and I was thankful. I climbed into my car and ripped out of the parking lot of the school heading to my place, I would have went to the gym but then X would expect an explanation from me which would result in him wanting me to move and I can't do that.

I got home and went straight to the gym not wasting time to wrap my knuckles. I swung over and over and over ignoring the pain from my skin ripping open. I can't believe that happened, I thought about what happened at lunch, everything was fine we were laughing and talking about tys fight but then I saw him. It had been so long that im shocked I recognized him, he was taller then I remember and he even had some stuble on his face. His eyes were still the same as was his hair. I was swinging at the bag over and over lost in my train of thought when I felt a pair of arms wrap around me and gently pull me into a wide chest. I knew who it was but the smell of cologne and confirmed who it was when he spoke

"Angel stop please..." he all but begged and his voice sounded so shaky and broken that it broke my heart, I slowly relax and he turns me to face him . I look up into his eyes and see so much concern and fear, he reaches down and gently grabs my wrists to examine my knuckle. when I looked down I saw both of my hands dripping in blood busted up pretty bad.

"Damn" he cursed under his breath as he dabs up the blood completely focused on my hands which were pretty numb at this point. "Come on." He said without giving me a chance to reply he turns and walks out with me silently following. When we got to the kitchen he remained quiet as he lifted me up and sat me on the contour making me suck in a breath from the surprise of it. I didn't know what to say to him and his emotions showing on his face were gut wrenching.

"you have been staring at me this whole time angel, it's distracting." Caiden said obviously trying to lighten the mood but he isn't good at hiding his emotions on his face right this minute. I sighed and looked around realizing it was just us here.

"Is it just you here?" I asked him and he paused on wrapping my hand for a second but quickly continued nodding.

"Tyler told us to give you some space so when they went to their classes I came here, good thing to cause as much as you love fighting if you would have kept going like that you could have done some serious damage Jay." he said sounding a bit irritated at the end of his sentence.

"yea that sounds like ty." I told him letting a soft smile touch my lips, he looked up at me for a second and tried to match the smile but it didn't meet his eyes. After he was done I hoped off the counter and went into the living room to sit down, I knew he would follow me and I knew we need to talk about what happened. Caiden walked in and sat next to me and without wasting a second he snaked his arm around my waist and scooted me into his chest so my back was laying against his chest and he nuzzled his head into the crook of my neck. I smiled at the sparks that shot up my neck.

"Are you ok?" He asked me making me shiver from his breath hitting my neck.

"Definitely Feeling better... are you?" I asked him as I closed my eyes getting pretty relaxed.

"I don't like seeing you hurt angel." he said slightly tightening his grip around me.

"Im sorry its just, I haven't seen jake for a very long time. After he handed me off to Marcus when my mom died he stayed away from me like I disgusted him. He ignored my screams and pleas and seeing him after all this time and after all I went through... it snapped something in me. He was suppose to protect me and take care of me, he was my best friend and though he never once layed a hand on me he definitely is the one who broke me. I should have wrapped my fists but I just wanted the memories of him to stop." we sat there in silence for a minute before he finally spoke.

"What are you going to do now? Do you believe he is telling the truth when he said he wouldn't tell anyone you were here?" Caiden asked me and I honestly didn't know what to say, I sighed heavily before answering him

"Honestly I don't know. I do not trust him but I can't shake the feeling he won't say anything. Even if he does I can't keep running. he saw you guys and If he tells marcus about you three then your in just as much as I am...which im so sorry for." this is all my fault and now My family is at risk, I should have stayed away from them but I was weak but I will protect them and im done running."

"Don't apologize Angel, I wouldn't change a thing about meeting you even if I could." He said making me smile and my heart flutter.

In that moment right there I felt no fear or pain, I only felt pure peace and I knew I would die before giving this up.

CHAPTER NINE: FOCUS

CAIDEN'S P.O.V.

"Look I really don't think this is a good move Jay, you have to many people from you past showing up and you need to stay hidden before someone finds out where you live." I watched as mike tried to reason with her but she has that stubborn bored expression stuck on her face.

"I am NOT loosing my title because I don't show up to this fight, im scheduled to fight and im fighting." She glared at mike who was running his fingers through his hair. Jay is scheduled for a fight tonight and with her brother, ex, and ex's brother showing up out of nowhere I think she needs to stay home.

"Babe I don't think she's gonna budge so cool off ok?" Stacy told Mike and we all knew she was right, Jay wouldn't budge.

"This is stupid." mike mumbled as he stomped out of the living room.

"I'll talk to him." Stacy told jay while giving her an apologetic smile and walked after mike.

"Just give him a minute to cool off he's just worried about you, we all are." Tyler piped up trying to help

"But he isn't wrong." I said making tyler sigh and jay's glare was locked on me.

"Dude don't..." Tyler asked looking at me almost pleading but Jay wasn't in a asking mood.

"Im fighting, if you guys want to be there then back me but don't try holding me back from my fights." She stated in a low commanding tone that I didn't know what else to say, she's fighting and I would rather be there and have her back then her be there alone. I nodded my head at her and she let the glare be replaced with her usual blank look.

" I'm going to train for a bit." She stated walking out of the living room not looking back at me.

"Hey! wait for me!" Tyler yelled as he jumped up and ran after her making me chuckle.

I ran my hands threw my hair taking a deep breath before standing up and walking into the kitchen. Mike and stacy were sitting at the table and luckily mike looked less agitated.

"I probably don't want to know the answer but did she possibly change her mind?" Mike asked when he notice me enter the room.

"Nope and she said if we keep trying to stop her from fighting then she will make sure we wont be able to get into the fight which means we wont have her back if something went wrong." I told him making him huff out a breath and shake his head.

"Of course she did, fine she wins I guess." Mike sighed and gave up before taking a bite of his food. Just then my phone went off and I look down to see its from an unknown number. I open my phone and all it says is

' Meet me at school. Midnight. Alone.'

I'm not sure who it was but when I asked them they never texted back.

"You good bro?" I look up to see mike looking at me with furrowed eyebrows and I quickly covered my confusion.

"Yea im good, I think May got ahold of mom's phone again and sent me a lot of emojis" I chuckled and luckily he laughed meaning he bought it. I don't know who it is but If I tell mike then he will tell tyler who will most definitely tell Jay and she has enough on her plate right now. I just needed to think this through and see where it leads before deciding to bring them into it. I walked out of the kitchen and to the gym to check in before heading home, when I got in there Jay and Tyler were already sweating and breathing hard, tyler was working on the punching bag and jay was on the treadmill.

"Hey im about to head out but ill see you guys at the fight tonight." I said giving them both a small smile, they both looked at me and nodded but didn't say anything. Tyler returned to punching but jay kept her eyes locked on me, I smiled at her and she returned the favor before finally braking eye contact to continue running.

â€¦

"Who are you fighting tonight?" Tyler asked Jay as we all sat in her changing room waiting for her turn to fight.

"A fighter named Detroit, should be an easy win. I read he got into a slight wreck eight months back because he was drunk and messed up his shoulder so this is a come back fight for him and that means I know his weak spot." Jay stated sending a wink to ty making him smirk, im definitely glad he is gay otherwise I wouldn't stand a chance. I really wanted to focus on this fight but my mind wouldn't stop racing with thoughts of the mystery text and my eyes wouldn't sit still as I searched the crowd half expecting someone to show up and try something. The fight ended up going as expected, Demon won and we all quickly left and went back to Jay, Ty, and Mikes home. Tensions were a lot better now that the fight was over and nothing happened but we need to figure something out otherwise We will be arguing every time she has a fight. Jay was currently doing laps in the pool with tyler and mike had already gotten out of the pool and was taking a shower. It was getting close to midnight and I was going crazy trying to figure out who the hell I was meeting, I decided that I might as well head that way and get this crap over with. I said my goodbyes and started to the school with my mind and heart racing.

What if this is a trap? Maybe I should have brought some back up or at least told someone where I went... No they said alone and the only people I could have told are the very people im hoping wont have to get involved. I pull up to the school and park in the back of the parking lot but hesitated before getting out of the car. I got this... I took a deep breath before getting out of the car and looked around, the parking lot was empty and it was dead quiet. Maybe this was a prank text or something. Getting out my phone to check the time it was five past midnight and there were no new messages.

"This is stupid." I mumbled to myself and turned to get into my car when someone cleared their throat right behind me making me spin back around quickly and jump a little. I was just looking this way and didn't see anyone, how did he get here so quickly, whoever it was had a black hoodie on covering their face but I could tell from their build that is was a guy, a large guy.

"Jumpy are we?" The stranger said in a deep but smooth voice.

"No shit. it is midnight, I have no clue who you are and you just appeared out of nowhere!" I snapped at the man who didn't seem fazed at all. "Who the hell are you and why am I here?" I asked in a low tone getting uneasy not knowing who im meeting with.

"I'll Take off the hood and tell you my name but before you react here me out...after im done if you don't like what I have to say then you can try your take in beating my ass." He stated smugly and I had a bad feeling I am not going to like this guy one little bit. After a second of thinking I nodded at him knowing I wouldn't be able to just walk away without knowing who he is and what he wants. The stranger took a deep breath before slowly reaching up and sliding his hood down and locking eyes with me. I felt the heat coming off my face and my fists clench just looking at his face.

"You son of a bitch." I spat at him and held myself back with everything I had in me.

"So I take it you know who I am... I suppose my sister has opened up to you guys." He smiled a little but I saw the sadness in his eyes.

"NO! You use to be her brother, you lost that title when you let your father Break her!" I yelled at him and I was loosing the battle with controlling my anger. I was surprised when that sadness disappeared and that same fire jay has filled his eyes

"That bastard is NOT my father!!" He snapped making me unclench my fists in surprise, what does he mean?

"Look I don't have long and Marcus is going to Expect me to check in. He sent me to follow up on leads and Find Jay he is obsessed and isn't giving up, I don't expect any of you to believe me but im not turning her over to him again, at the time back then I thought it was safer but now I know she would have been better off killed then what they did to her...she use to be so full of life and laughter. One day I hope she will let me explain to her what happened all those years ago but for now she is going to need you guys." He paused for a minute as if lost in thought and for a second I could see a tear rolling down his face.

"Why did you want to meet me, how did you even get my number?" I asked getting uneasy with the Compassion I was starting to feel for him, in my opinion he didn't deserve it.

"Marcus isn't going to stop looking for her and I need you to know that if he finds her then you need to get away from her, far far away." He stated matter of factly and my anger rose once again.

"The hell I will!" I spat at him officially ready to swing

"Calm down! If marcus finds her he will take her back and if she is going to make it then she needs to be strong but if he finds out about you boys then He will kill you three just to break her fighting spirit and I will lose all chances of her forgiving me so please just do this for her." He all but pleaded with me, I locked my eyes on his and thought hard.

"Is that it?" I asked him with a blank face, he nodded his head but doesn't say anything. I walked up to him and before he got a chance to say anything I swung a decent right hook making him stumble back a little grabbing his face.

"Fine, I will do what is best for Jay but that doesn't mean you and I are cool. Don't NOT contact me again and if Jay wants you gone then you better get the hell out of this town." I gave him one last glare and turned to get into the car and leave. This was definitely something I needed to think about and im not sure if I should tell jay or not. ill at least tell her about marcus but im not sure how she is going to react to me meeting up with Jake, God I hope that she doesn't kick my ass.

JAY'S P.O.V.

Im sitting on the back patio trying to wrap my head around everything Caiden just said and I got to say im not doing so well at it. All I can do is stare at him and watch as he shifted uncomfortably in his chair from my lack of words. I'm not sure how long it has been since he stopped talking and though I have no clue what to think about what jake said I do know that Caiden is a fucking moron.

"Please say something, im getting anxiety." Caiden said trying to smile but he was to nervous for it to look real.

"Training room Right now." I said in a low stern tone making him even more nervous. I didn't wait for him to reply as I got up and walked to the Gym room. When we got in there I wrapped my fists silently and Caiden just stood in the corner watching me looking scared to death.

"Would you relax already im not going to hurt you." I snapped at him knowing he was worried about me kicking his ass but I don't think I could if I wanted to. All I really want to do is protect him but he made it painfully obvious that I can't always do that.

"Then what are we doing here?" Caiden asked sounding more confident then before but still didn't walk up to me.

" Look what you did was stupid as hell, meeting some stranger in the middle of the night all alone I don't even know what you were thinking. you made it painfully clear that no matter how much I want to, I can not protect you â€¦ Any of you, but the least I can do is train you to protect yourself." as I finished I turned and looked at him only to see him smiling at me like a crack head.

"What!" I snapped yet again at him but he only smiled wider.

"After everything I told you the thing that upset you the most was the fact I was unprotected...you care about me Jay moore." he smirked at me making me scowl. Of course I care about him but his ego does not need the boost.

"Ha more like upset that if something happened to you then tyler and mike would team up and end me, wouldn't want to loose my boys now would I?" I smirked back at him and he laughed shaking his head.

"Whatever you say angel." he sighed as he walked up to me and started wrapping his wrists.

We trained for about two hours and by the time we were done he was laying on the couch unable to move due to his sore and throbbing muscles which definitely made me laugh.

"I don't know how you do it Ty... she worked me like a dog bro." Caiden said to tyler who was stuffing his mouth full of pie.

"Bro..." Tyler started but paused to chew his mouth full of food. After he finished chewing he looked back at Caiden. "Your dumbass deserved it." he finished making me send an 'I told you so' glare at Caiden. Mike and tyler were just as upset by his actions as I was we get he was looking out for us but he could have gotten hurt and that isn't ok.

"Still, I don't think im going to be able to walk for a week." Caiden mumbled closing his eyes

I let out a chuckle before walking outside to think. It's hard to process everything Jake had said to Caiden, I mean I can't figure out his endgame here. He hasn't told Marcus of my whereabouts yet but that doesn't mean he wont I just don't know what he is waiting on, it's not like he hasn't turned on me before so what's different now?

"Hey you ok?" I jumped and turned to see mike , I didn't hear him come outside.

"Honestly, I don't know." I sighed before pushing the chair next to me with my foot for him to sit in. He took the seat and turned to face me.

"When Ty and I first started bouncing around we ended up staying with our uncle first. Everything started off alright, we had a bed and food but he started drinking pretty bad. One night I was coming home from a football game and when I got there Uncle Kenny was on top of Ty just beating him over and over...There was so much blood. I got home in time to save tyler but I don't think Tyler has fully gotten past it. A few months later Kenny tracked us down and begged for forgiveness on his knees crying but we didn't trust him so we just walked away. That same night he killed himself, the reason I told you this is because I know my uncle was a good man but the alcohol changed him...I don't know what drove Jake to hurt you the way he did but I do know that if I could ask my uncle what drove him to drinking...I would." By the time Mike finished I had tears running down my face and my heart was pounding.

"I didn't know that....Thank you for telling me mike I think I know what I need to do now." I wiped my tears and got up giving him a hug before walking through the house and straight to the front door.

"Hey where are you going?" Tyler shouted as I grabbed my keys and opened the door.

"I need to handle something, ill be back later." was all I said before shutting the door and walking to my car... No more running.

JAYS P.O.V.

I knew I needed to talk to X before I did anything. He needed to be filled in on what is going on and I need his advice on what to do. his first response will be to run but I cant do that, I need his next best advice. I got to the gym and took a deep breath before walking in, as i scanned the room i found X training one of our members on the back mat. As i walked up to them they both stoped what they were doing and Xaiver gave me a smile.

"We need to talk now." i stated in a tone letting him know this was serious and his smile fell only to be replaced by a hard expression but i saw the fear for that split second in his eyes. he nodded his head before following me into the office. X closed the door and took a seat behind his desk but did not saying a word just watching me intently.
I proceeded to tell him about what all has happened, Jake showing up at the school, me beating the crap out of him, Caiden being an idiot and what jake had said and lets just say i could see the steam coming out of his ears by the end of it all.

"ARE YOU FUCKING STUPID!!! HOW COULD YOU NOT TELL ME ANY OF THIS! DO YOU WANT TO GET CAUGHT BY MARCUS???" He yelled as he took a breather to punch his desk.

"Will you calm down! Do you think i enjoyed getting beat everynight, being starved and broke all because of my brother? Don't you think i have thought about what im risking by staying here? X i love you but you are all i have had since i was just a child, i have done nothing but shut people out and fight and move...though i had you i was still utterly alone but now i have Tyler, and Mike, and Caiden...they are my family and it feels good having them in my life. Jake clearly knows about Caiden which means if i take off...they are all alone. i don't want to run anymore, i was made into a fighter and i think its time i actually started fighting, but i need you to have my back, to support me X. Your my rock." i looked up at him with tears in my eyes and he instantly relaxed. he stood up and walked over to me and wrapped his arms around me while i just cried.

"Shh Jay, i understand and if its finally time to stop running then i will back you... i just don't want to loose you. your my little girl, i see you as my daughter and all i ever want is for you to be safe." he said as he held me tighter making a small smile spread across my face.

"Thank you." i mumbled as we pulled apart and i wiped my tear stained face.

"So what now?" he asked as he flopped down in the chair next to me.

"Good question." was all i answered because honestly i have no fucking clue.

"Well how about a fight? You set up your fight with Raider to be a tag team fight and its around four months away, which means you and tyler need to be training and fighting together... at least some of yalls fights." He stated and i nodded my head because he has a point.

"So i got you two your first tag team fight set up for tomorrow night." As he said this i jerked my head up to look at him and he smiled at the excitement in my own smile.

"Who are we fighting?" i asked knowing there weren't any local tag teams.

"Honestly im not sure, their manager or whatever wouldn't tell me their names but its a tag team so either way you guys will get good practice together." X shrugged his shoulder when he said this then got up and walked to the door.

"You and Tyler go get ready, i have to train Daniel...he's been slacking on his knockout times." Was all he said as he walked out. i know he was putting on a show, making himself look calm and levelheaded but i also knew that on the inside he was a raging storm, mixed with fear, pain, rage and revenge...and that scared me.

â€¦

"Tyler! You home?" I called out as I walked into the house, it was quiet for a second but then i heard a lot of stomping coming from upstairs and before i knew it Caiden, Tyler, and Mike were shoving eachother as they ran down the stairs almost falling as they reach the end of the stairs with Stacy and Rafal following behind them shaking there heads at the boys acting crazy.

"Where have you been!" Mike shouted

"What happened to being smart and staying safe!" Caiden yelled

"Are you ok?" Tyler asked with worry in his eyes as they all pulled me into a bone crushing hug.

"Drama queens." I heard Rafal whisper making Stacey snicker and tyler glare at him

"Are not! We were worried." Tyler defended them as they finally released me allowing me to breathe.

"You three have been loosing your minds since she left." Rafal smirked at tylers glare

"Yea you guy's have been in full blown panic ready to track down jake and torture him till you found her!" Stacey stated making my eyebrows shoot up, i knew they cared but i didn't imagine they would of gone that far if something were to happen to me. It warms my heart so much to have them care for me like this but at the same time it makes my blood turn to ice because this is exactly why i could never leave if marcus found me...They would end up in danger even if marcus didn't know about them because they would find him.

"You guys need to chill, im fine just went to talk to Xaiver i felt he deserved to know what has been going on so he isn't blind sided." I told them as i made my way to the Livingroom and plopping down on the couch. Caiden sat right next to me on my right and i leaned my head on his shoulder, the smell of his cologne calmed me down a little bit but all in all today has been really stressful. Tyler sat down on my left and i layed a small pillow on Caidens lap before laying my head in his lap and putting my legs in Tylers lap, Mike and Stacey sat in a rycliner and Raider sat on the other side of tyler. We all stayed just like that for a long minute. Caiden rubbed my head gently as i let my eyes close.

"Are you going to leave?" I heard Tyler ask barley loud enough for me to hear but i heardit. i opened my eyes and looked around only to notice all eyes were on me. They all looked so sad and scared at the thought of me leaving, including Stacey. i Gave a warm smile and closed my eyes back.

"I Would never be able to leave you guys, You are my home." i said and i felt tyler and Caiden instantly relax, i knew they were worried about my answer.

"Plus it sounds like if i were to even leave you would find me anyhow, might as well save you the danger and the search." i smirked and heard everyone laugh knowing it was true.

"We would go to the end of the world for you Angel." Caiden said and though i had my eyes closed i knew the look he was giving me, it was the same look that made my insides burn, the same look that stops time and at the same time make my whole body feel like a storm, He was looking at me with up most Desire and compassion...The same way i look at him.

CHAPTER TEN : FAMILY
CAIDEN'S P.O.V.

"So who are you guys fighting anyways?" i asked jay who was sitting next to me on the couch with her head laid on my chest and eyes closed. I can't help but smile as i think about how far we have come, Day one she wanted nothing to do with me and now she is comfortable enough to let me hold her. Though i would love to have more with her but i know that i need to let it happen on her terms at her pace.

"Not sure but im not worried i got a badass partner in that ring so they don't stand a chance." she replies with a victious smirk on her face

"you ever get a fighter you are worried about fighting?" i ask while shaking my head at this crazy women's pride.

"Raider...he is my equal in that ring, that fight will be the one that scares me." she replies and i feel her shiver which makes me instinctively hold her tighter. I decide on changing the subject, i don't want her having to be stressed because of him or any of them. These past few weeks have been one nightmare after the other for her and she needs some peace, that's when a horrible yet good plan comes to mind.

" So i actually need a favor tonight. I need you to come to dinner at my place tonight."no sooner then the words left my lips Jay shot up and stared at me looking horrified with her eyes wide and jaw hanging open and i couldn't hold back the smirk.

"Before you freak out let me explain, my mom wants to meet who im constantly hanging out with when i usualy just stayed home before you came to town, you don't have to but it would make her feel better and would mean a lot to me." by the time i finished i wasn't sure what she was thinking, i saw fear and confusion written all over her face.

"Caiden...i don't know...i haven't really met anyones â€¦ i don't think she would like me." she stuttered for a second looking flustered before she looked down at her fingers, so fucking cute.

"Trust me, she will love you...its impossible not to." i smiled at her and she snapped her head up locking eyes with me, i realized i had in other words said that i loved her and felt my face heating up, i looked away and chuckled saying

"I mean look at tyler you take one backroad with the kid and he is all about you, protective and non trusting." at that i hear her laugh and turn to look at her, shes relaxed and obviously not even thinking on what i had let slip out but what scared me was i didn't even realize i felt that way i mean...i do though i don't know how or when but i fell in love with her.

"Okay, ill go." she smiled at me and felt my heart sore

"Awesome ill let her know." i smiled and sent my mom a text

' Hey Jay said she could come to dinner tonight at the house
so if you want to meet her nows you chance.

p.s. no funny business mom. '

no sooner then the text is sent my phone rings and its my mom, oh my god this women.

"Ill be right back." i tell jay as i slide off the couch and walk towards the kitchen.

"Hey mom" i say as i answer and walk out of the living room

"Don't hey mom me, are you messing with me? it not nice to play tricks on your mom you know?" she asked sounding like a mad women and i couldn't help but laugh

"Im serious, unless you don't want to." i state with an evil smirk plastered on my face

"NO! i want to, tonights perfect ill have food ready by seven, no six. six will work, oh i got to get started i love you got to go bye!" She rambled out and hung up before i could reply, this women had lost her mind, i knew this would be horrible for me but now im seriously scared. I walk back into the living room but my heart drops when i scan the room and Jay isn't there. i hear some shuffling upstairs and head toward the sounds which were coming from jays room. I knocked on the door

"It's open!" she yelled and i opened the door to find her in her closet throwing clothes around.

"Um what's going on?" i ask cautiously as another piece of clothing fly's across the room

"What am i suppose to where? seriously im asking i have never done this before." she states not even giving me a glance as she shuffles through her closet.

"You can where whatever you want, don't worry youll look good either way angel." i state with a smirk because of how paniced she is over wanting to look good to meet my mom. she spun around and glared at me

"I don't want to look good, im meeting your mom dude! i need to...just... you know what! you are no help get out and find Stacey and meg!" she yelled frustrated and spun back towards the closet. i couldn't hold the laugh in any longer so i hurried out and muffled my laughs with my hand before heading off to find the girls.

JAY'S P.O.V.

What the hell has happened to my life!! this isn't what i do, i do NOT meet parents and i do NOT meet the parents of the man who i have definite strong feelings for, and who all but told me he loves me yea! i didn't miss that but he clearly didn't mean to say it and im definitely not ready to confront any of those feelings.

"Hey girl..you ok?" i hear meg say hesitantly behind me and i turn just in time to see Stacy dodging a dress i threw just seconds ago.

"Shit sorry stace. no im not you know what i must have lost my mind! agreeing to this stupid crap like meeting his mother! i have nothing to wear... what do i wear!?" i all but yell at them and they look stunned. they slowly walk up to me and each grab one of my arms before pulling me to the bed.

"Sit we got this." Stacey said before they turned to my closet.

"Maybe i should just cancel this doesn't feel right." i say feeling every nerve in my body vibrate.

"You are not canceling your just nervous." Stacey says as she rummages through my clothes

"Yea girl just breathe, life hasn't been easy but this...this will be a piece of cake compared to your past." Meg said with a warm smile before both of them appear infront of me with Stacey holding a simple red tanktop and my plain black leather jacket and Meg was holding a pair of my black jeans and white sneaker...simple yet perfect. i eventually got to telling meg and danny about my past it just didn't feel right hiding it from them and Stacey got the story from mike night one. They were supportive and sad and danny was livid and has been a clingy protective, a lot like Tyler but i don't really mind.

"oh my god i love you guys!" i jumped up and gave them a hug before grabbing the clothes to change into making them giggle.

"So now that im all set up, wanna talk about you and danny?" i ask narrowing my eyes at meg who went white

"Wha..What?" she stutters now turning red as a tomato

"Oh come on help me out stace." i say looking over to a smirking Stacey

"we all see it meg and you two both love eachother, we are just waiting for one of you to make the move." Stacey said and meg lets out a sigh of defeat and flops down on my bed.

"well tell him that...i have loved him since we were six but its like he doesn't see it and i cant risk our friendship f there is a chance he doesn't feel the same." meg replies sounding so defeated that i couldn't help but frown...she was scared and had been waiting a long time.

"Maybe i can get Caiden to figure out where his head is but not let him in on whats going on that way if he doesnt, which is a massive if, then you can at least start moving past him and focus on you." i say giving her a small smile and she returns it.

"You think that would work?" she asks with hope filling her eyes and i nod before giving her a hug which Stacey joined in on.

"Love you guys" Stacey said

"Love you" meg and i replied at the same time making us all laugh.

â€¦

oh my god, i can't do this. i have been sitting in his driveway for about five minutes unable to get out of the car, he wanted to pick me up but i pushed for me to drive here. i know they know im here i saw the curtain move several times since i pulled up but i cant make my feet work, im scared. after a few more minutes and the curtain moving one more time i slowly get out of my car and take a deep breath as i approach the front door, as i get to the door i stop and hear Caiden in the house yelling something to his mom about spying out the window at me and i cant help but smile. That smile fell quickly when i knocked on the door and it opened immediately.

A tall women with dark hair and silver eyes stands on the other side with a wide smile and a little girl hiding behind her legs

"Hello Dear please come in! you must be jay." She said as she urged me inside and shut the door behind me.

"That's me, uh nice to meet you. you have a nice home." i said not sure what to say here and still debating running for it.

"Oh aren't you sweet. This is May, Caidens little sister." she said and i smiled down at the little girl . She had the same piercing blue eyes Caiden has and dark black hair.

"Hey there" i say smiling at the little girl, she still doesn't say anything as she studies me unsure if im to be trusted. Lucky for me i was warned about his little sister and Mike gave me a helpful tip. i reach into my bag i brought and pulled out a Nutella filled cupcake and her eyes lit up as she ran out from behind her mom.

"Now youll have to talk to your mom about when you can have it but a little birdie told me these were your favorite." i said with a small smile as i passed the cupcake to her mom who had a big smile on her face.

"Thank you!" may yelled and gave me a big hug

"Looks like you already won over May" i heard Caiden say and i look over my shoulder to see him sitting on the stairs watching us, has he been there the whole time?

CAIDEN'S P.O.V.

She has been sitting in her car for about five minutes parked in the driveway but not moving. I heard he car when she pulled up as did my mom, we peaked out the window as she was pulling into the driveway and my mom has been peeking back out the window every forty-five seconds to make sure she hasn't left yet.

"Mom will you please stop creeping out the window and just be patient, i told you she isn't use to meeting people, shes shy." i mumble the last half and i hear the knock on the door that i have been waiting on but before i can even stand from the stairs my mom has the door open pulling her inside with meg around her legs. I sit there and and watch as she talks with my mom, poor girl looks terrified but she's killing it at the same time. I watch as she brings Mays favorite thing in the world out and can't help but smile, how'd she know.

"Look's like you already won over May." i say with a smile and watch as she looks over her shoulder and her eyes meet mine, i seem her relax instantly and a true smile appears on her face as relief feels her eyes making my world melt. I noticed my mom smile even wider so she must have picked up on Jay relax because of me.

"Had some help." she smiled back as she walked over to me. I got up and walked towards her before softly grabbing her hand and giving it a reassuring squeeze making her relax even more and i slowly led her to the kitchen.

"The food smells great." Jay said giving my mom a soft smile before sitting at the table, i had all intention of sitting net to my angel but May beat me to it. i gave her a small playful glare and she stuck out her tong at me.

"May hun why you don't come sit with mommy so Caiden can sit with his â€¦ friends." She paused before saying friend and gave me an evil smirk.

"But i wanna sit next to her!" May pouted and crawled into jays lap clinging to her like a monkey. Jays eyes got really big for a second but she quickly relaxed and wrapped her arms around may letting a smile land on her face.

"Actually i would rather sit with you anyways may, you seem way cooler." she told may who giggled and wiggled back into her own chair

"Hey!" i said as i plopped down in the chair across from her and pouted which made jay laugh and may giggle. The first like fifteen minutes went perfect as we all ate and talked. I could tell my mom really likes her and may clearly does too.

"So Jay you haven't mentioned much about your family, do you have any siblings?" My mom asked and my head snaped to jay whos knuckles were turning white as she gripped her fork and her face was pale white. I shoot a serious glare at my mother because we talked about not mentioning her parents before jay got here.

"What i didn't say anything about her parents, oh shit." my mom said as she covered her mouth with her hand and gasps, she turns and looks at jay "I'm sorry sweetheart." she said and i sighed before lowing my head.

" Um its fine really, its not something i would really like to get into but your a very sweet women and you are obviously a good women because of how well Caiden turned out..." i look up at her while she continues to speak and i smile at the confidence on her face.

"so i will say that i had the most amazing parents, my father was the kindest man i have ever known even at age eight i knew how amazing he was. He was my superhero, he was also a MMA fighter towards the end of his career. he died not long after my eighth birthday, my mom now she was feisty, a forse to be reckoned with but she was a mom ya know... sweet and always knows the right thing to say but she passed when i was nine. as for my siblings i had a older brother he was...Magic. He was my protector...from the bullies and the monster under my bed. He is gone as well, leaving me with the family i have made here, Tyler, Danny, Mike, Meg, Stacey, Caiden." as she finished my mom was blinking back tears and so was Jay, hell i was too.

â€¦

"Thank you for coming over Angel, it means a lot" i said as i walked her to her car, Dinner ended happier once we got past moms Bad Conversational skills in there.

"Thank you for inviting me it was actually really nice, your sister is awesome." She said as she opened her car door but instead of getting inside she turns around to face me

"I still think im cooler." i said with a smirk

"If you say so" she replied. i was about to reply when she surprised me by getting on her tiptoes and softly placing her lips on mine, it was quick but i swear in all its cheesy glory there were fireworks.

"Goodnight Caiden" and with that she turned and climbed into her car

"Night my angel." i whispered back but i knew she heard it because i saw the smirk on her face

My Angel

CHAPTER ELEVEN : UNLEASHED

JAY'S P.O.V.

"Tyler give it a rest already, you need some energy for tonights fight." I say for the third time in the past four hours trying like hell to get him to stop training, he is really on edge about our first team fight.

"Yea babe other wise your gonna sleep through the fight." Rafal smirked making tyler stop and glare at him

"I'd never." was all tyler said before hitting the bag one more time and coming over to sit next to me, the fight is in a few hours and honestly it has been bugging me that we don't know who we are fighting but its driving Ty insane.

"Still no word on who we are fighting?" Ty asked as he wiped the sweat off his face and neck with a towel.

"Ty, you know that if i knew so would you. Relax we got this." i gave him a smile and checked my phone again just to be sure, nope nothing from X.

"HEY! I brought pizza!!!" I heard Mike shout and tyler and i were on our feet in a second racing and shoving to get there first with Rafal laughing behind us. We rounded the corner and when mike saw us his eyes got huge and he tossed the pizza on the table and leaped out of the way.

"HA! i win i beat you!" I snickered at tyler and stuck my tung out like a child

"No way i did!" Tyler protested and reached for the box off the table as did i

"Caiden help me out!!" i yelled as tyler and i had a stare down. Caiden had just entered the locker room

"Sorry Ty, she's right." He winked at me and i snatched the box away from tyler

"Bull you only sided with her because your all goo goo eyes for her." Tyler snapped at Caiden

"Oh shush" Caiden snarked and shot tyler an eat shit glare and i smirked as i shoved a piece of pizza in my mouth then passed the box to ty.

"Demon!" I heard X yell from down the hall

"Lazy ass" i said making the boys chuckle

"I heard that!" X yelled

"Shit!" i pouted as i walked out glaring at the guys who were now on the floor laughing. I walked into

X's office and he had a look on his face that usually meant he just got into it with someone and it didn't end to well for him.

"Sup X?" i ask as i plop down in the chair

"You Guy's are fighting the reaper twins." X started to speak but i held my hand up to stop him.

"Hold up...let me get the guys in here otherwise imma have to repeat all this like 50 time... BOYS I NEED YOU!!!" I roared as loud ass i could and just as i expected all three of them busted through the door within seconds of me calling, all looking for the harm that made me yell like that and i couldn't help but chuckle.

"Easy there now, Xaiver has some news and i didn't want to repeat it over and over to yall." i said with a shrug of a shoulder. Tyler laughed but mike and Caiden glared at me

"Ever heard of a phone call instead of giving us a heartattack?" Caiden asked but i saw him trying to hide a smirk.

"This was quicker anyways, its about the fight." When i said that all three of them snapped their heads to Xaiver. Tyler sat next to me and Caiden stood behind me while Mike sat on the couch.

"So?" Tyler asked obviously having enough of the anxiety

"You two will be fighting the reaper twins, they aren't that popular anymore but when they use to fight it was always nasty. Those boy's fight dirtier then most underground fight's allow, the last fight ended up with them in prison and they were just released a month ago...you two are their return fight and i don't know if this is such a good idea, but i do know they will fight dirty and i do know there isn't anything i can say to talk you two out of it but be careful." by the time Xaiver finished i only had one question.

"What did they go to prison for?" i asked not really wanting an answer, X took a deep breath before locking eyes with mine.

"They killed two other fighters during their last fight, they were about to loose and pulled a blade. Killed them both before anyone knew what was happening." Xaiver looked away and rubbed his face. Tyler can't be in this fight, it would be on me if he dies.

"X is right, maybe this isn't a good idea." I said not really wanting to see Xaivers Expression right now because its gotta be bad, i have never not faught...NEVER.

"WHAT?! you not fight what the hell is happing?" Xaiver was laughing now and i shot him a death glare that shut him up.

"ENOUGH! Tyler could seriously get killed in this fight and i brought him into the fighting world so that is on me, and i won't let him get killed." i stated making everyone silent

"She really does care about you boys..." Xaiver mumbled.

"Jay i know your gonna look out for me but i need this fight ok... i need to know that i can have your back too. We know what to look for, We got this." Tyler said making me look into his eyes, they were almost pleading me for this fight.

"FINE! but if you die on me then im going to kick Rafal's ASS" i stated making tyler's eyes go wide

"And ill help" Mike said folding his arms.

"Fine but if you die then ill kick Caiden's ass and you know i can do it." Tyler smirked at me

"And ill help" Xaiver pitched in and i stole a glance at Caiden who was looking a little pale now

"Deal, but this refers to any of our tag team fights." i smriked and Tylers smile grew.

"Deal." He stated

CAIDEN'S P.O.V.

I don't like this, i don't like this at all. Not only can i loose one of my closest friends but also the women im sort of secretly in love with, but i can also get my ass pumbled by tyler and xaiver. I left the Gym to clear my head while Tyler and Jay went back to practicing and planning and watching some of their old fights, i went to the Beach and sat just out of reach of the water.

"Hey you good man?" I heard a voice that i knew all to well now.

"What are you doing here Jake, Jay's pissed enough you showed up at her school and talked to me plus i don't want you anywhere in my town or near her." I stated not bothering to spare him a glance. I heard him take a deep breath before coming and sitting about three feet to my left.

"Damn, i guess i never really expected her to care about anyone the way she does you guys. I'm happy for her though i just wish i could help somehow." i heard him say and my fists were instantly clenched

"You wanna help, then fucking leave! Do you know how broken she is because of you and you alone! Do you know she doesn't sleep more then four hours a night because of nightmares you guys gave her! Do you know how long it took for her to let me even stand near her without her backing away! If you magically started caring now then the only thing you can do is take your sorry ass out of this town and never let Jay see your pathetic face, become dead to her because that's what she needs now." i shouted and by the time i finished i was breathing heavily but he didn't so much as flinch. He slowly lifted his head and he had tears streaming down his face.

"You don't understand, i .. it doesn't matter. i'm leaving town and wont be back unless marcus plans to head this way, I wont let him get her again and i can tell she has all the family she needs to keep her safe and happy. the number i texted you off of is how you get in touch with me, only you have that number but if she gets in danger or is found then call me...i'll handle it." he stated as he stood up and turned to walk away.

"We will protect her, i promise." i told him, i don't know why but somehow...someway i truly believe he cares about what he did and about her i saw it in his eyes when he looked up. he stopped walking but didn't turn around.

"Do better then i did." was all he said before walking away and i couldn't help but wonder what reason he was going to give me for not protecting her. I sat there for a little while longer before deciding i need to head to the gym before the fight starts. As i pull in i notice that people have already started to arrive. I park my car around back and use my keycard to get in through the back door, im glad Jay gave us all one of these so we don't have to fight the crowds. I walk into there joint room and saw tyler talking to rafal and mike on the couch while jay was putting on her jacket and mask.

"You guys ready?" i asked gaining their attention and they all look at me but my eyes stay firmly on Jay beautiful eyes.

"Born ready" She remarked giving me a wink and i smiled as my heart raced.

"Where did you run off to bro?" Mike asked as i walked over and took a seat in the empty chair next to the couch.

"Just went for a drive, no biggy." i lied. i didn't want to mention what happened earlier because last time jake talked to me it really put Jay on edge and she doesn't need that distraction before this fight. As if sensing her gaze i looked up and kind of wished i hadn't, the look on her face made it perfectly clear she knew i was lieing but after a second of looking at eachother she looked away and adjusted her ponytail...she didn't ask. i couldn't help but smirk at the thought of her knowing me so well, it means she has been paying close attention to me and that makes me feel incredible.

"Time to fight..." one of the stage guys said and walked out. Tyler and jay nodded to eachother and we all headed down the hall stopping behind the curtain.

"We are gonna go on ahead so we can get right next to the matt in case anything goes wrong." I said gaining a stern nod from Mike and Rafal.

"You got this guys, be safe." mike said and we headed to the matt

"LETS GET THIS FIGHT GOING WITH OUR FIRST TAG TEAM THE REAAPPPEERR TTWIINNSS!!" As Xaiver yelled their ques the twins walked down the isle and to the mat. They were gruff looking both about six foot tall and medium build. one has a shaved head and red beard while the other has red short hair and a five o'clock shadow. They both had tattoos covering their arms and the one with a shaved head has an eyebrow piercing.

"AND FACING THE NEWCOMERS IS THE HOUSE FAVORITE, OUR CHAMPION AND HER PARTNER DEEMMOONN AND BEEAASSTT!!!" When Xaiver said their names the whole building went insane which only pissed of the twins on the mat. Jay and Tyler walked down the row and to the center of the mat, they did their team signature facing eachother and locking hands before pressing their foreheads together they then faced the crowd and gave them a stern nod.

"SAME RULES APPLY AS A REGULAR FIGHT, TAP OUT OR BLACK OUT ALL FOUR FIGHTERS ARE NOT TO LEAVE THE MAT

TILL YOU TAP OUT OR...BLACK OUT. READy, STEADY, FIGGHHHTT" Xaiver roared, here we go.

JAY'S P.O.V.

Tyler and I knew we were ready we had spent all day mentally and physically ready for this fight. Underground tag team fights were different from legal tagteam fights, in the underground fights all four members of the teams fight at the same time on the same mat. Basically like a group fight. Xaiver signals for the fight to start and exits the mat. Ty and I got into our stance and had our eyes trained on their every move, I ended up fight the twin with the read hair and Ty is facing the bald twin. My twin kept his position but not taking his eyes off of me, I noticed from the corner of my eye the bald twin started side stepping to the left heading behind us. Tyler was watching him intently though and made sure to keep his eyes on his competitor. Snapping out of my thought the guy im facing takes a small step towards me making my focus snap back to him. They are trying to distract us so that the other can attack from behind and as if confirming my thoughts I felt tylers back to mine and I smirked...nobody is attacking either of us from behind.

I noticed that the guy im facing was trying to figure out a new strategy and I took this as my chance. I twisted my body with force and delivered a kick to the right side of his face making him fall to the ground and a little stunned. I noticed I no longer felt Ty behind me and glanced back to see he had also stated his attack at the same time and had the other twin backed into the corner. Checking on tyler proved to be a bad idea because as I turned back I was caught with a brutal left hook making me fall to the ground and within seconds this guy was on top of me punching my stomach hard over and over. I managed to shake the pain and wrap my legs around his neck. instantly his hands were grasping my legs trying to get out of this hold. I mustard up all my strength and slammed my legs as fast and hard as possible to the ground making sure his back and head hit the ground under my ankles.

I jumped up and took a couple steps back to pull myself together, I saw tyler out the corner of my eye but from what I could tell he was doing just fine and I can't afford to get distracted again. I noticed my guy standing back up and I was instantly in a fighting stance, I need to trust my partner and make sure I do my part. I advanced on my target and started throwing jabs as swiftly as I could he dodged the first but I made contact with the second. I gave a swift jab to his stomach and another to his right cheek making him stumble back and when he looked into my eyes I saw the same look marcus always gave me. He looked over to his brother who was about knocked out with tyler punching him furiously. His eye's snapped back to me and for a second I felt like I was in that cell again with marcus coming straight for me, I was so stunned that I hadn't seen the guy reach behind his back and pull out a small blade and before I knew what was happening he was right in front of me and had the blade slicing into the right side of my cheek.

I snapped back to reality with the stinging of my skin being sliced open, I caught his wrist with the knife in it right before it was able to slice my throat and with as much force as I could use I twisted his arm behind his back and kept twisting until the blade fell from his hands and I kicked it away. Suddenly he sweeps his leg under my feet making me fall hard backwards and once again he was on top of me delivering one blow after the other, two to the face one to the stomach anther to the face. I felt my blood covering my face and it was making loose strands of my hair stick to my face. One more blow to the face and I would be out, there was no way for me to get out of this. I glanced to the side and saw Caiden and mike with wide eyes and fighting and trying to get to me but security is holding them back, I also notice that Xaiver was being held to the ground by who I recognized as the twin's security. My attention returned back to the man ontop of me as an evil smirk appears on his face as if knowing it will only take one more hit.

As his fist was drawn back I gave in but refused to tap out so I simply locked eyes with the man about to strike but instead of hitting me he was ripped off of me with so much force that he flew across the mat I looked up half dazed to meet tylers eyes but instead I looked up and was met with a pair of light green eyes that I did not recognize. The stranger had brown shaggy hair and had tattoos covering his arms. he gave me a nod then turned his attention to the man he just ripped off of me, he charged at him and hit him left and right over and over until blood was flowing from his face and he was on the verge of passing out but before he did the green eyed man lifted him from the ground slightly and with venom in his words he said

"Now nobody likes a cheater." and with that he headbutted him hard enough to hear a crack and dropped him to the ground, unconscious. I look over at tyler and he is walking over to me with his twins passed out behind him. he helped me up and I went to take a step back to gain my balance but pain coursed through me and a started to collapse. I saw tyler reach out to catch me but before he could I felt myself being lifted up and carried off the mat. I looked up to see the green eyes guy smirking while he carried me towards the curtain and the crowd was going insane. I looked over his shoulder and saw tyler looking pissed, Mike looking confused, Caiden looking furious, Xaivier punching one of the men that was holding him down before turning to look at me worriedly and all now hurring my way. I wanted to climb out of this guys arms but in all honesty I was in to much pain to even more and I couldn't tell what hurt more, my face from the cut that got wider from the punches it received or my stomach from the repeated blows, either way I was in no mood to fight mystery guy plus I wanted to know why he saved my ass...he kind of looks familiar now that I think about it.

CHAPTER TWELVE : GUESS WHO'S HERE

JAY'S P.O.V.

He carried me to Xaivers office and quickly but very gently he laid me down and ran back to the door closing and locking it but also locking the deadbolt. Normally that wouldn't be that bad but after a break in last week X replaced his office door with a heavy duty metal door and I was barley able to move locked in the room with some guy who wants God know's what.

"Why did you lock the door?" I asked sternly trying not to show how much pain I was in as I sat up from a laying position, I don't want his guy to think im easy prey. He turned around and held up a finger telling me to wait and seconds laster there wasalot of banging and yelling from the other side of the door and though I couldn't understand the words I knew who it was. The guy infront of me smirked and pointed his thumb over his shoulder at the door.

"That's why, I needed to talk to you for a minute alone before your people invade our privacy." he said as he made his way to me. As much as my instincts told me to get up and don't let him get near me I knew that I wouldn't be able to hide the pain im in from him so I sat very still with a emotionless expression.

"What do you want?" I asked the question that was running through my mind the most. he smiled and sat down in the next to me.

" don't recognize me do you ? Well I did just save your ass maybe a thank you that would be a good start." he chuckled and sent me a wink'

"No I don't recognize you dude and please I had that guy and if not then beast would have got him no problem." I glared at him but I must have also looked confused because he chuckled before speaking

"yea it sure looked like you had that guy, you looked like a dancing ogre out there getting your assed kicked." after saying that his smile grew and my breath hitched in my throat, it couldn't be... only one person has ever said that exact thing to me.

"Jackson...?" I asked almost a whisper as tears filled my eyes. I looked into those green eyes that I haven't seen since I escaped.

"The one and only, do you know how hard it was to find your ass?" he chuckled but I couldn't move, I couldn't speak, and all of a sudden I couldn't breathe. before I was in a full blown attack the crashing of the office door had us snapping our attention to the doorway and in came a dangerous looking Tyler, Caiden, Mike, and Xaiver ready to kill.

"Well that didn't last long." I heard Jackson say as he stood up and I snapped my eyes to him, he sent me another wink before turning to face the boy's.

"Gentleman thanks for taking such good care of my little bluejay, but how is it I was in the back of the crowd and was able to save her yet you guys were where? oh not you Magic X I knew you would have been there if you could." At the sounds of his nickname Jackson gave him when he was just a child Xaivers expression soften and he stepped infront of the boys.

"Jackson boy, is that really you?" X asked and when Jackson nodded Xaiver enveloped him in a massive hug while the boys were looking a mixture of confused and pissed.

"Somebody want to tell us what the hell is going on?" Caiden asked fuming with his eyes locked on Jackson while Tyler had his eyes locked on me. he walked around Caiden and mike straight to me. When he got to me he bent down infront of me and grimaced as he examined the gash on my face.

"Damnit jay...im sorry I wasn't there in time." Tyler all but chocked out and as I looked into his eyes I saw the tears he was holding back.

"Hey â€¦ you did your part, I was so busy worrying about you that I really wasn't paying attention...this is on me." I said and even though I was in so much pain I ignored all of that and pulled myself up to pull Ty into a hug that he and I both needed. The room was suddenly silent and I looked up to see everyones eyes on ty and me. Everyone then headed to where ty and I were. Tyler quickly sat on my left so he could clean my cuts, Jackson took the seat to myy right earning a death glare from Caiden but Jackson just smirked at him at Caiden sat on the couch opposite of us with mike while Xaiver knelt down infront of me to examine my injuries.

"what happened out there?" I asked looking at Xaiver, referring to them being restrained.

"Before the knife got pulled out we saw him panicking and thought he was going to try something like that but when we tried to get to you their group or whatever attacked us... we were out numbered. I have never been more scared in my life Jay." Xaiver said making my heart clench, I could see the fear in him still.

"I'm ok X." I told him but ended up grimacing because ty was cleaning the wound.

"Sorry." tyler said

"Good thing I was there huh bluejay?" I heard Jackson say and I turned my head to see him smirking.

"Okay that's it who The fuck is this prick?" Caiden spat getting seriously irritated but once again Jackson only smriked at him.

"This is Jackson, its a long story really but his mom worked as a maid in Marcus's house...his bio dad is marcus but they don't claim eachother. Jackson was aloud to stay in the servents building but he had to fight as well to earn his keep. When I got there he was about ten and still in training, Marcus had us train with eachother because of being the same size and speed, we trained everyday together and he use to sneak me food and water, bandages, medicine, and even books at one point. We were bestfriends and he hated jake as much as I did when he heard it was jakes fault I was in that mess, I never thought id see you again." I Said with a bright smile as I looked at Jackson who had a smile to match.

"Yea after you left I have so confused, I was happy you got out safe but terrified of what marcus would do if he found you not to mention I missed the hell out of you. As soon as I got old enough I got the hell out of that place and have been looking for you every since I got out o there, your a hard women to find you know that? Hell I followed one clue to the other even to that sorry ass raider then remembered how much you talked about finding you small town marcus wouldn't think to check for out in California when we were imagining your escape growing up so I bounced from one small town to the next going to every fight I could find and it was pure luck that I found you here because I almost didn't show with it being a tag team fight but when I saw you fighting I knew... I knew I finally found you." Jackson finished and gave me a proud smile.

CAIDEN'S P.O.V.

"So if he's Marcus's son does that make you two siblings through jake?" I couldn't help but ask hoping they would say yes because there is no way I could compete with a childhood love bonded together by trauma.

"No not really but Jay and I were eachothers family back then, before Xaiver before anything or anyone we had eachother ." Jackson answered but im still not completely sure there isn't something there, maybe im just being to jealous.

"Speaking of Jake, you heard anything from him?" Jay asked and I tried really hard not to tense up, what if Jackson knows Jake has been talking to me?

"You know I have nothing to do with that piece of shit, luckily im better at finding you then he is tho last I heard from mom marcus has been livid that jake hasn't found you yet." Jackson stated making me relax, not only because that means he doesn't know jake was talking to me but also because that means he was being honest about keeping her location from marcus.

"Actually hotshot, Jake already found jay before you." mike said and I couldn't help but smirk knowing he doesn't like this guy either.

"WHAT! and your still here why?" Jackson yelled as he jumps up from the couch.

"Because I can't keep running but according to you he hasn't turned me in to marcus and its been a minute since I beat the shit out of him." Jay said with a smirk and jacksons jaw dropped.

"You luckily brat! I have been dieing to do that since we met" Jackson said making jay laugh but stop quickly and grabbed her stomach.

"You ok angel?" I asked making her look up at me and smile and Jackson looked at her wide eyed.

"You let him call you angel?" He asked with shock written all over his face.

"shut up." She glared at him making me smirk and him break out into a wide smile

"That makes so much sense! He was all ' who is this prick' and territorial. so you two are dating?" Jackson laughed out and I almost laughed at how quickly jay turned red.

"Not dating shut up before I kick your ass." jay snapped at him making me chuckle.

"Yea ok." Jackson smirked at her before looking over at me.

"give her time, she will cave. she is definitely into you." Jackson smirked at me making me instantly like him a bit more and jay slapped him upside the back of the head making him yelp and everyone else laugh.

"I wanna go home, lets catch up more there." jay said making us all nod in agreement. Tyler and I helped Jay get to the passenger side of her car after much protesting and I got in the driver seat.

"If you crash my car ill fucking butcher your car!" Jay snapped at me making Jackson chuckle from the backseat.

"I'm not going to mess up your car now relax." I told her but she still kept a glare on her face.

"I can't believe you got your dream car." Jackson said making her smile a little.

"Of course I got her, she was waiting on me as well." Jay smirked

"Hey uh, Jackson." I said as I glance in my rearview mirror as see him looking up at me.

"I just wanted to say that I didn't mean to sound like an ass earlier its just a lot of people have resurfaced from jays past and you are literally the first one that wasn't here to cause her more harm ." I stated feeling good about putting my pride aside.

"What do you mean a lot, who else has found you Jay?" Jackson asked and I could hear the tension in his voice.

"Raider, Brad, and Jake." Jay answered practically whispering as she shot me another glare.

"Son of a Bitch so im pretty much last to find you im lucky you stuck around, shocked to be honest." Jackson asked in aggravation.

"Yea I am to, before I moved here all I did was hide, fight, run, repeat. Then I moved here and no matter how much I wanted to keep to the pattern these people in this town just dug their way into my life and if I were to leave then they can get hurt. This is my home I need to protect it." Jay stated plainly with a shrug of her shoulder and I smiled knowing that she definitely made it hard to be in her life.

"I'm happy for you BlueJay." Jackson smiled at her but when I looked in the rearview mirror I noticed that Jackson looked like he wanted to say something but stopped himself, I wonder why.

JAY'S P.O.V.

Finally made it home and lucky for Caiden he didn't hurt my baby otherwise it would have been war. I started to wobble towards the front door ignoring everyone protesting.

"Jay will you please just let us help?" Tyler asked but threw his hands up to surrender when I shot him my best death glare.

"Still so fucking stubborn." I heard Jackson mumble behind me making me smirk. Before I even got halfway to the door I feel someone pick me up bridal style and as I go to protest I look up to be met with Caidens icy eyes and all my words vanished in my mind. I decided not to fight him and instead I welcomed his warm embrace that slowly made my pain float away.

Caiden carried me all the way to my bed and gently laid me down and stacy came in to help me get cleaned up and dressed because I couldn't do it on my own. Afterwards Caiden came back in and proceeded to carry me all the way to the living room and laid me on the couch and I slowly lifted my head so Caiden could sit down and I could lay my head in his lap. Tyler stood from his seat and came to sit under my legs and gently laid them back down in his lap, my whole body was killing me. We all talked and I think as the night went on the boy's loosened up to Jackson knowing he means no harm.

I don't know when but I ended up dozing off and when I woke up I could have sworn I heard screaming but everything was silent now, I was covered and sweat shaking. I took notice of my surroundings while I tried to calm my heartrate, I was in my room. Suddenly the Door burst open and Jackson came running in with a worried look on his face.

"What's going on are you hurt?" He asked panic in his voice as he quickly sat on the edge of my bed.

"What...What are you talking about?" I asked but my words were a little shaky.

"You screamed Jay, I was right across the hall...what happened?" He asked making realization dawn on me, the scream I heard was me.

"I.. I didn't... I didn't know I screamed, I had another nightmare." I said bringing my knees to my chest, they are getting constant and I keep seeing the look on caidens face when the gun goes off.

"What was it about?" He asked in a soft tone as he crawled into the bed with me and wrapped an arm around me to hold me, I have missed him.

"I really don't want to talk about it." I told him

"Come on bluejay, you know you can't burry it inside you talk to me you use to." he stated as he rubbed my head

"I...I'm standing in a field Marcus, raider, and jake are standing across from me, suddenly Marcus has a gun and he point's it next to me and when I look... Caiden is standing there, then the gun goes off and everything goes black." I tell him as I feel my heartrate slowing down as he holds me.

"You really do care about him don't you?" He asked in an even tone

"Yea I do, please don't mention my nightmare to anyone." I told him in a sleepy voice as I felt my exhaustion kick in.

"Don't worry I will help keep him safe bluejay, you just get some rest. I got you." He whispered and within seconds sleep swept over me.

CHAPTER THIRTEEN : NERVES

CAIDEN'S P.O.V.

It's been a couple day's since the fight and though Jay is feeling a lot better she still was at home resting while all of us have to be in school, I almost envy her because I don't want to be here. I made it through my physics test and when lunch came along I was starving!! Tyler, Mike, and I got to the lunchroom and today was pizza day so we paid extra for double slices, well Tyler paid with some of the money he earned from the fight. After getting our food we made our way to our usual table and sat down.

"so what do we really think of Jackson?" Mike asked as he took a bite of his pizza.

"Honestly im not so sure, I mean hes a cocky prick but he seems to have Jay's best interest in heart." I said with a shrug.

"Yea I mean if Jay trusts him then I guess we should, she doesn't trust easy." Tyler added in making us nod.

"Speaking of the prick, here he comes." Mike said nodding his head behind me and I turned to see he was right, Jackson was here and coming straight towards our table with a smirk on his face. he got to the table and sat next to me flopping his tray on the table.

"What's up boys?" He asked with a smirk, Mike, Tyler, and I looked at each other then at him.

"When did you start here?" Mike asked before I got the chance to.

"Today "He replied simply before biting into his pizza.

"So how long will you be in town?" I asked making him look up at me and smirk.

"Will you relax already?" He asked never letting the smirk leave his face.

"What?" I asked furrowing my eyebrows together

"Oh please you have been marking your territory since I got here but I get it. Look Jay is completely into you and I see you are into her just as much, I'm not here to mess that up. Me and her are a lot like her and Tyler, family plus if it makes you feel better I am taken. I have been with the same women since I was fifteen and after I make sure Marcus is dealt with so jay and I are safe then im gonna marry that women and start a family." Jackson said making me shocked honestly I didn't think it was that obvious but I guess it is.

We all talked for a few minutes but I wanted to step outside and call Jay to check in on her before lunch ended. I got up to leave and made it halfway to the door when I heard my name being called out.

"Hey Caiden wait up!" I turn to see no other then Zach standing about three feet in front of me.

"What's up Zach?" I asked sounding annoyed because I honestly don't like the prick

"Not to much, hey how have you been?" He asked with a shrug

"Fine, now if you'll excuse me" I stated boredly and turned to leave but didn't get a step in when I heard what he said

"Actually how's that sweet piece you boy's have been playing with." Zach said and I spun back around to see him smirking. I see Zach's best friend freddy step behind him smirking with a couple other guys and before I knew it Tyler, Mike, Danny, and even Jackson were all behind me in seconds.

"What did you say Anderson, I don't believe we heard you correctly from our table?" Mike said comly, a little to comly to be honest because that was the quiet before the storm.

"Oh the boy's and I were just wondering if you guys wouldn't mind letting us know when your done playing with the new girl so we can have our turn." Freddy smirked at us and all hell broke loose with Tyler, go figures, taking the first punch at freddy. I immediately went for Zach while Jackson, Mike, and Danny went for the other three it looked like a riot with all of us fighting and everyone was shouting and pulling their phones to record us. Mike and I ended up switching guys after I got a few good licks in on Zach because I knew he really wanted a few punches himself after warning this asshole.

Wasn't long before a whole group of teachers were fighting through the crowd to us and pulling us apart. It took a few minutes but they were able to separate us.

After waiting in the office for fourty-five minutes my mom showed up and after examining my busted lip and bruised cheek she went into the principles office and I just waited knowing I was at least suspended but they wont expel me if she has anything to do with it. Not long after entering his office my mom came out with a blank expression and motioned for me to follow her. We stayed silent until we were at her car then she turned and gave me her best ' spill it ' look making me smirk.

"They had some very ugly things to say about Jay, Tyler started it but any of us weren't going to just let them walk off after what all they said." I said with a small smirk and shrug while watching her closely. She kept a blank face before smiling and giving me a hug.

"Now that's my boy, but what did I say about getting caught?" She smirked at me as she pulled away from our hug and turned to get in her car.

"Got to go it's almost time for may to get out of school. Love you." She said as she climbed into her car.

"Love you too mom." I replied and watched as she drove off before turning to get into my car which Tyler and mike were already waiting for me at as well as Jackson.

"You boy's get suspended as well?" I asked and they all smirked and nodded.

"Need a ride to Jay's?" I asked Jackson and he shook his head no.

"I got my own ride but I appreciate it." He said as he Patted the Motorcycle parked next to my car.

"Didn't know you ride, it's a nice bike." I stated admiring his Motorcycle.

"Yea I learned when I was fourteen, right before Jay escaped...She use to love it when Marcus let he get out for an hour a month and I would take her for a ride...of course followed closely but nun the less I know she always wanted to learn hell she probably did by now." He smirked as he grabbed his helmet.

"See you boys there." Jackson stated receiving a nod from all of us and as he drove off we climbed into the car.

"Okay maybe not a prick but the dude's still cocky." Mike said making us all laugh in agreement.

JAY'S P.O.V.

It's been a little over a week since Jackson got here and besides the fight they had at school about God knows what thing's have been quiet. It's actually been pretty nice to relax but Jackson is still acting weird like he is hiding something but I can't get him to slip up yet. My body still hurts but it is to a point that im use to and can handle, I started back training a few night's ago, I told the boy's it was because I needed it to heal which isn't a lie but it's also because Xaiver has a meeting for me to attend and told me to be ready in case things go south but I don't want to tell the boy's till last minute so they won't waist time trying to talk me out of it.

I sneak up on Caiden before he walks into the house and tap his shoulder.

"Hey hold up." I whispered so nobody inside would here.

"Hey Angle what's up?" Caiden whispered back with a smirk when he saw it was me

"I need to talk to you alone for a minute." I said and nodded for him to follow me. We walked silently out to the tree line before stopping and facing each other.

"Okay what's Jackson hiding?" I asked with my no bullshit glare drilling straight into him.

"I don't know what your talking about Angle." Caiden replied making me roll my eyes.

"Fine don't tell me." I stated coldly as I walked away back towards the house, he may be able to keep his mouth shut but I know who will tell me what I need to know.

I walked into the house and waisted no time

"TYLER!!!!" I yelled as loud as I could to make sure there was no way he couldn't hear me. As usual within second's tyler is in front of me as well as Mike and Jackson all looking panicked.

"What's going on Jay?" Tyler asked with wide eyes

" I need to talk to you." I stated keeping a blank face but before I could walk away Caiden came running inside catching everyone's attention.

"Don't say nothing Ty!" Caiden all but shouted earning a glare from me

"Huh?" Tyler said looking a mix of confused and worried.

"What's going on?" Jackson asked making me cut my glare to him.

"You that's what. I want to know what your hiding and don't say nothing because I know better and I also know tyler is the only on who WON'T keep shit from me." I stated matter - of - factly.

"Ohhhhh you mean that." Tyler said and this time it was Jackson who glared at him and Ty just smirked back.

"Don't you dare." Jackson warned but tyler only smiled more.

"Jackson has a girlfriend he plans on marrying." Tyler said smugly and the confusion only grew for me.

"Asshole." Jackson hissed.

"That's it. That's the big deal...this is good news why wouldn't you tell me?" I asked feeling a little hurt.

"Because I know you Jay and I am not going anywhere until Marcus is no longer a issue and I know that if things were to get worse then you'd try to make me leave but I can't...it isn't safe for Rachel not until he's gone." Jackson said and I didn't know what to say, not because he was wrong but because he was right. If marcus shows up I would try to make Jackson leave but the thing is, I will do that with all of them regardless of if they have families or not because they are my family.

"You really think you being in love would make a difference? Do any of you think that? Let me tell you four something, no matter what connection I have with ANY of you, when the time comes I plan to handle my fight with Marcus and the only one who remotely will get away with being there when it happen is you Jackson because you were put through some of the same shit by marcus. Now stop keeping secrets from me and let me make my own DAMN choices." I stated before storming off to the gym but stopping to give them all one last glare as if daring them to follow or object to anything I just said.

CAIDEN'S P.O.V.

I watched as Jay stormed off to the gym no doubt and I returned my glare to Tyler.

"I thought we weren't going to say anything to her?" I asked accusingly

"She asked and im not gonna lie to her, not for him or anyone." Tyler said with a shrug and a smug look on his face

"Suck up." mike smirked at his brother. Jackson sighed and turned to leave down the hall.

"Where you going?" Tyler asked

"To the gym, we all know that's where she's at and I need to talk to her." Jackson stated before disappearing down the hall. Tyler was of course following after him because he doesn't like that guy, he say's it's because he doesn't trust him but I think he is just a bit jealous of jay's bond with him. After a few second's tyler came running back in here smiling wide.

"You guys got to see this they weren't even talking for a few second's and now they are fighting... she is kicking his ass." Tyler laughed and we ran down the hall to the gym. When we got in there sure enough Jackson was pinned to the floor and Jay was on top of him punching him.

"Still think I need protecting?" She smirked as she threw a left jab to his abdomen

"What's going on?" I asked making Jay look at me, I noticed Jackson smirking and I knew he is going to use this distraction to his advantage. As if reading my mind rolls them over and is now straddling Jay and he punched her twice in the abdomen.

"Yes I think you need back up because you obviously have distractions here that you care about and that can get you killed." Jackson smirked back as she struggle against his grip.

"And you don't have distractions? Someone you love who you need to protect no matter what, no matter how painful or dangerous it is for you to protect them? Someone that you would die for just so they wouldn't have to feel any of the pain we felt? Yes you do...guess that means you need protecting too."

Jay said with a tone sounding almost defeated but that didn't stop her from sending a right hook to his jaw and knocking him off of her. I tried my best to ignore the feelings swarming inside of me, the way she said all of that made it seem like she was talking about herself at the same time but there was a sadness to her when she said this.

She got up and held her hand down to help Jackson up, I look at tyler who was still smiling and I can't help but roll my eyes at this idiot, I look at mike and he has a sort of pained and sad look in his eye that worries me.

"What is it Mike?" I asked but he didn't look at me just kept his eye's fixed on jay as she walks up to him with furrowed eyebrows.

"When Marcus show's up your not going to leave to save yourself from getting taken are you?" He asked making a mix of emotions run through me, some fear of her leaving but mostly guilt that if she stays it is because of us.

"You know I can't do that mike." She said with an almost apologetic look in her eye's.

"Your not going to let us help you when he show's either are you?" He asked and I didn't even want to hear the answer because I already knew it, and it wasn't going to work with any of us. She glanced at me really fast and I couldn't read the emotion in her eyes before she was looking at Mike again.

"It isn't safe plus ill be to distracted if you guys are there." She replied not sparing me another glance.

"You won't be able to stop us." Mike said in a cold tone that made me flinch and without another word he turned and walked away.

"He isn't wrong." Tyler stated before walking after his brother, Jay sighed before rubbing her hands over her face.

"Can I have a second to talk to her alone?" I asked looking at Jackson who had a busted lip he nodded and walked out.

"Did you two always handle disagreements like that." I asked making her smile a little but not nearly enough to convince anyone she was ok.

"Yea, last punch wins the disagreement." She stated sounding once again defeated. I walked over and sat next to her on the bench.

"Angel look at me please?." I asked whole heartedly and she did without any hesitation.

"I know this is all new and scary to you, to have people and a home to loose but you need to understand that Tyler and Mike aren't any different. Me and you are all they have and they are terrified of loosing you, we all are. They didn't have a home or much of a family besides me until you came around, now there's a chance that someone we care a lot about might get taken from us and you wont let us help. Train us, but please Angel don't fight this battle alone because you don't have to anymore." I told her and at this point she had tears streaming down her face. I pulled her into a hug and let her cry as I rubbed her head.

"I'm so scared." She cried harder then before after saying that and it broke my heart.

"Shhh I know babygirl, we all are but we got you like you have us." I told her as I held her close to me.

"I'll never let them take you Angel, I promise." I stated confidently because that is a promise I will never break.

CHAPTER FOURTEEN : GETTING THERE

JAY'S P.O.V

I have been training the boy's now for a minute and though I have stopped fighting them on having my back, I have decided it's best to focus more on getting prepared for the fight's to come rather then focus on the feeling's I have for Caiden. I think it's safer that way all around but I can't deny that what I feel for him runs straight to the core of my heart. The fight with raider is this Saturday and Tyler and I have been training non stop and because there aren't a lot of tag team fighters out there we trained with mike and Caiden or Xaiver and one of his fighting buddies which worked out well for training mike and Caiden as well.

"You alright?" I turn from the punching bag to see Jackson standing behind me.

"Yea just blowing off some steam what time is it?" I ask as I turn back to the bag and return to training.

"Time for the guy's to get home from school any minute, why didn't you go today?" Jackson asked me as he came to sit down on the bench across from me.

"Same reason as you, need to be ready for what's to come and school's a waste of time right now." I shrugged

"I guess that's as good an answer as any." He said with a smirk making me roll my eyes and suppress a smirk. I just nodded and continued training, this fight with raider has me on edge. I'm really worried that if he wins then im either gonna have to take off or go with him but if he looses I have a feeling he wont stick to his end of the deal.

"I still think I should be fighting with you instead of tyler." Jackson stated once again today even though we have been over this a dozen times.

"The hell you Say Jackson!" Tyler's voice boomed through the gym making me spin around to see a upset looking tyler.

"I said that I should be the one in the ring with Jay not some Newbie." Jackson snarked back

"How about me and you go a few rounds and see who fight's like a newbie prick." Tyler spat back and at this point they were inches from each other fists balled up.

"All i'm saying is I have been doing this a lot longer and know how to fight alongside jay." Jackson stated as he took a deep breath trying to control his temper.

"And you think I can't have her back?" Tyler said letting his rage lace every word.

"Clearly not or do you not recall what happened at the tag team fight a little bit back?" Jackson smirked

"Enough you two or ill fight alone. we have been over this Tyler is my partner in my tag team fights. We started this team together and that's how it's gonna be so stop antagonizing him Jackson and tyler whatever your issue is with Jackson I suggest you get it straightened out or ill bench your ass." I glared at both of them before walking out of the gym to get something to drink, and maybe to see if Caiden was here.

"Hey Mike." I smiled at him as I walked to the fridge. I grabbed a water and looked around the Livingroom and kitchen.

"He's outside on the phone." Mike stated making me blush a bit, I didn't think I was being that obvious.

"Don't no what your talking about." I said trying to hide my blush with my hair.

"Why don't you two get together already? You are both crazy for eachother but neither are doing anything about it, kinda like meg and danny use to be... glad they finally got past that crap and started dating." Mike said before taking a bite of his sandwich.

"It's just not the right time ok, I care about him but until I know the danger is over with I can't risk his life more then I already am." I told him but when I looked up he wasn't look at me but over my shoulder, I turned around to see Caiden leaning on the frame of the doorway.

"How long have you been standing there?" I asked turning redder then before.

"Long enough to know ill get my chance to be with you eventually." He smiled back at me and I turned to give mike a eat shit look when he started laughing at me.

"how's training going?" He asked as he walked to the table to sit down.

"I think we will be ready but if Tyler and Jackson don't stop fighting then I may end up being down a teammate." I sighed and leaned against the countertop.

"What are they fighting about now?" Mike asked also getting tired of this. They have been fighting since day one and I don't know how to stop it but it's getting old fast.

"Jackson doesn't think Tyler is enough to back me in the Fight with Raider and Tyler is pissed that Jackson thinks he can back me better then him." I huffed out and mike sighed while Caiden just shook his head.

"I'll talk to Ty see what I can do." Mike said and I sent him a thankful smile.

"I appreciate that but I think I have a better idea." I smirked and nodded for them to follow me. I walked into them gym when Tyler and Jackson we having some kind of stare down.

"Alright this shit has got to stop. both of you get your gear and get in the car...your gonna fight it out." I stated and turned to leave. As I walked past a smirking Mike Caiden wrapped an arm around my shoulder and walked with me.

"Pretty smart Angel" He whispered in my ear before kissing me on top of my head making fire erupt within me, I don't know how much longer I can hold back.

CAIDEN'S P.O.V

We drove silently all the way to the gym, well sort of silently ever now and then Jackson or Tyler would make some snide remark to the other about how bad they were gonna loose but jay soon ended that with a threatening glare and turning up the music. I got to admit Jay never stops surprising me since the day I met her, I mean bringing mike and tyler into her home, being Demon, Getting tyler's inner Beast out, Getting mike and Stacey back together, making me fall in love with her, and now finally gonna put an end to these two's fighting all the damn time.

I get where Jackson is coming from but at the same time he has no right to say Tyler can't defend jay. Yes The fight with those twins got out of hand but Jackson hasn't fought along side Jay in a long time where as Tyler has been training with her for months now and would be the better choice in the fight with raider I just hope Jay's plan actually works. We all got out of the car but before heading inside Jay turned to face Tyler and Jackson.

"Here's the deal, you two will fight underground rules and though I think Tyler would be my best bet for this fight with raider im sick and tired of the constant arguing so I'm giving you both the opportunity to Prove yourselves. The spot for my partner has opened up so when we get inside and set up you two will fight, knock out or tap out, winner is my team mate in the fight this weekend no argueing that's final now let's go." Jay stated firmly and I can tell this not only shocked but irritated Tyler but he pushed it aside and looked at a smirking Jackson.

"No problem." Tyler winked at Jackson and followed after Jay and I just chuckled and caught up to my girl as Jackson followed.

We got inside and Jay spoke to Xaiver, I knew he liked her plan by the smile on his face and he followed us so he could watch the fight. Tyler and Jackson got changed and set up in the middle of the mat, For Jay's sake I hope Tyler wins this otherwise she's gonna be accomplishing the opposite of what she wanted to today because the fighting will get worse.

No sooner then She signaled for the fight to start Tyler charged from his corner towards Jackson and Jackson swung his leg around to kick Tyler in the abdomen but before he made contact Tyler dropped to his knee's and slid across the floor leaning back as he slid under Jacksons leg. As soon as Tyler had gotten behind Jackson he Jumped to his feet and spun around giving three swift jabs to Jackson's mid-back making him stumble forward. Tyler then kicked the back of Jackson's left leg making him fall to the ground.

Tyler went to attack again but Jackson Quickly rolled onto his back and used both his feet to kick Tyler in the stomach hard enough to knock Tyler down into the right corner. Jackson was on his feet in seconds and standing infront of tyler delivering two jabs to his stomach and one to his face then I Saw Jay tense up and I could tell she wasn't wanting tyler to loose this fight. Jackson went to give a right hook to tyler but Ty caught Jackson's right arm and headbutted him hard making Jackson stumble back enough for Tyler to get out of the corner.

At this point they were both bloody and breathing hard so both of them stood in a defensive position three or four feet away catching their breath but not letting their eye's leave eachother. After a minute longer Jackson made the first move charging Tyler and when Jackson was no more then a foot away Tyler jumped forward into the air with his fist balled and drew back, when his feet made contact with the ground he also made contact with a brutal punch to jacksons lower left jaw making him once again fall to the ground.

Jackson tried to pull himself up but wasn't fast enough because Tyler was on top of him punching left right left right again and again to Jackson's face and their was blood everywhere. One more hit like that and Jackson was going to black out for sure, I look at Jay and I see relief and pride cover her face making me smile. Looking back at the mat Tyler Grabs a weak and almost unconscious Jackson by the throat and bring's his fce a few inches from his own.

"Enough Bullshit, I'm Jay's teammate and I am more then capable of taking care of her." Tyler smirked before slamming Jackson's head down and punching him one last hard time in the face making Jackson pass out.

"That's my boy." Jay smiled as she said this and walked toward's tyler.

"Never doubted you Ty." She mumbled as they brought their foreheads together and his smile couldn't have been.
bigger.

"Now help Jackson and tomorrow we train all day because the real fight is coming up." She said before turning to leave the mat and talk to Xaiver.

JAY'S P.O.V.

As I look around all I see is grass and tree's, I'm in a field but not sure exactly where. Looking around I see Marcus, Jake. and Raider, this all seem's familiar but I can't place it. I see jake yelling something to marcus and raider look's fearful. I turn and see marcus pointing a gun at me and I sense of realization kicks in.

" Shoot me ill die before I let you take me back." I said feeling even more sure this has happened before. Marcus looked at me for a second before smiling.

"Oh i figured as much but will you let him die?" He stated with a smirk before pointing the gun to my left but when I looked my heart dropped because right next to me was Caiden. Next thing I hear was the hammer of a gun being pulled back and everything went black with a gun shot ringing threw the darkness.

I pulled myself from the thoughts of my nightmare as I slowed down the treadmill needing to take a break, I turn to see Tyler sparing with Jackson and im glad the bickering slowed down, though I am hoping eventually it would stop all together.

"Imma go get something to eat you guy's want something from the kitchen?" I ask Tyler and Jackson and they both shake their head's no. They have both been on edge with the fight being tomorrow night and haven't had much of an apatite. I walk into the kitchen to find Caiden making a sandwhich and I smile at his timing.

"Wanna make an extra one? I'm starving" I smile as I sit at the counter. He looks up at me from his sandwhich and smiles before sliding it across the counter to me.

"Actually Angel this one was for you" He winked at me before grabbing a cold water and handing it to me.

"Thank you." I smiled at him before drinking some of the water and starting on my sandwhich.

"You ready for tomorrow?" He asked as he sat down in the chair next to me. I shrugged and took another bite of my food before answering his question.

"As ready as we are gonna get, time's up." I said because honestly im not to worried but at the same time Raider is a damn good fighter and his brother has a temper when it comes to fighting plus with Tyler being the one who kicked his ass in school that day he is going to make this fight personal.

" Mike said Tyler barley slept last night." Caiden said making me nod my head.

"Yea I couldn't sleep either, neither could Jackson so we ended up training most of the night." I said having another flashback of the nightmare I have been having. My heart drops thinking about the look on Caiden's face before the gun went off and a shiver runs down my spine.

"Hey you ok?" Caiden asks placing his hand on mine and when I look into his eye's I can see the concern he has for me.

"Yea just nerves." I say giving him a warm smile which he returns, we stay like this looking at eachother silently and I notice he is hard in thought about something before he quickly glances at my lips. A flashback of the nightmare hit's me again and I cleared my throat as I stood ignored the irritation I felt towards myself for stopping what was about to happen.

"I should probably get back to training, thank's for the food." I said sending him a wink before walking towards the gym.

"You'll be the death of me angel." I heard him mumble as I walked out of the room and though he wasn't being literal I felt a sharp pinged in my chest and I could only hope he isn't right.

CHAPTER FIFTEEN : IT'S TIME

TWO DAY'S BEFORE FIGHT...

JAY'S P.O.V.

After training as hard as we possibly could the guy's have finally convinced me to take a break from training and have some fun. After arguing for a while about what to do we finally decided a simple day at the beach would be perfect.

"Ok what all do we need to grab for a cookout? What exactly do you make at a cookout?" I asked as I skimmed through all the food in the store. After not hearing a reply I turn to see the guy's giving me a questioning look.

"Have you never been to a cookout?" Mike asked and Caiden smacked him upside the head

"Ow, sorry." Mike replied looking down while he rubbed the back of his head.

"No I haven't." I answered but smirked at the glare Caiden was giving mike.

"Burger's and Hotdog's are most common, sometimes steak." Tyler said dropping a box of hamburgers and two pack's of hotdogs into the cart.

"Sound's good to me now all we need is drink's and we are good right?" I asked while we walked down another isle filled with chip's and other snack's.

"Well We still need some snack's and buns for the food then some drink's." Caiden said throwing some chip's into the cart. I nodded and grabbed some cookies. After we finished getting everything we needed to which was a lot more then I thought we headed towards the beach. When we got to the beach Meg, Danny, Jackson, Stacy, and Rafal was already their getting the grill set up well Danny and Jackson were getting the grill set up, the girls we putting on sunscreen. We hopped out of the car and headed to the grill area carrying the food we had just bought.

"Hey just in time, the grill is about ready." Danny said giving me a hug while Jackson grabbed the bag's from my hand.

"Thanks." I smiled at him and walked over to the girl's. I took off my top and short's to reveal a simple red one piece bathing suit. Most girl's prefer a two-piece but im not a fan of walking around in underware for the world to see.

"Thirsty?" Meg asked and I turned to face her to see her holding out a energy drink called K.O (knockout) which I found ironic given my career, I smiled and took it as us three girls walked toward the water.

"So how are thing's going with you and danny?" Stacy asked meg making meg instantly smile wide.

"Really good actually, I was worried at first that it would be awkward going from friends to dating but it feel's natural ya know?" Meg asked as we sat on the beach towels they had already laid out.

"That's how you know it's right, take mike and I for example we went from dating to avoiding eachother at all cost's for a long minute then when we start dating again it was effortless. it was like breathing â€¦ just natural." Stacy finished and I couldn't help but watch Caiden laughing with the guy's by the grill probably about something stupid while she said this.

"I think Jay know's what we mean." I heard stacy say making me turn to face them only to see them both smirking at me then looking at Caiden then back to me.

"Yea I know exactly what you mean." I said simply before turning to give Caiden another glance only to find his already looking at me, he smiled at me and I returned a smile to him. Just then Caiden look's behind us and his smile fall's as he head's straight to us with fire in his eye while the boy's suddenly get deadly serious and head this way as well.

"Well hello love." A voice behind me said making my entire body tense as I slowly turned around.

CAIDEN'S P.O.V.

Today was meant to be perfect, we had the food and we had some badass waves yet all that goes out the window as I stand no more then a foot away from Raider.

"The hell are you doing here?" Tyler spat at him before anyone else got a chance to ask.

"Just enjoying the day out before our fight." Raider replied with a shrug but his eye's never leave Jay who is right behind me.

"Well go enjoy your day somewhere else, you aren't wanted over here." I stated in a warning tone making him lock his eye's with mine and smirk.

"You don't stand a chance with her, you'll never be able to protect her... you aren't even her equal prince charming." He stated smugly making my blood boil and my fist's clench.

"Watch it." I Heard Mike say from behind me.

"At least we aren't the one's causing her pain, can you say the same?" I asked crossing my arm's over my chest. I watch as he take's a deep breath before answering.

"Maybe at one point but I'm not going to make the same mistake's as before." Raider replied once again looking at Jay.

"No just going to find other ways to hurt her." I glared at him as I said this.

"I think it's time you leave us be, we are trying to have a decent day out and can't do that with you here but hey make sure your brother is ready for another asskicking." Tyler stated earning a glare from Raider while Jay just stay's quiet behind me during the whole confrontation.

"I will see you tomorrow love." Raider said winking at Jay who glared at him in reply which only made him chuckle as he turn to walk down the shore line away from us.

"Asshole." I mumbled before turning to face Jay who was staring blankly at Raider's retreating form.

"You ok Angel?" I ask as I pull her into my arm's. She nodded but didn't say anything as I held her watching Raider disappear on the shore line.

" Let's just enjoy the rest of our day, it's beautiful out here." I say pulling her towards the group over by the grill. Since we have met Jay our group of three turned into a big family and honestly we are all a lot happier then before. We decided to enjoy the food before getting into the water and besides Tyler burning the hotdog's everything turned out pretty good. We ended up staying at the beach until it got dark before finally heading home and I enjoyed seeing both Jay and Tyler loosen up a little bit and not worry about this fight even though we had a rough start with Raider showing up it got better after he left, it did however make it painfully clear how real this fight is tomorrow.

JAY'S P.O.V.

I watch in the mirror as a bead of sweat run's down my forehead causing goosebumps to line my arm's, the fight is in about thirty minutes and I feel like my chest is getting tighter and tighter not allowing me to breathe. If we loose this fight will he honor our deal and leave me be or will he do something worse? A flash of Raider standing next to Marcus in my nightmare makes a shiver run down my spine. What about Brad, he is already dangerous enough and now that Tyler has beat him once before makes this personal which makes Brad even more dangerous, Tyler can get seriously hurt here tonight and if he goes down then I won't win this. I will do everything to protect him even if it means tapping out of this fight if he goes down, but I don't think ill be able to honor my end of the deal if we lose.

"Breathe Angel" I heard Caiden whisper in my ear as he rubs the goosebumps on my arm's till they disappear.

"We won't let him take you, I won't let anybody take you." He whispered and stopped rubbing my arm's when the goosebumps vanished but he didn't remove this hands from my arm's. I took a deep breath to try and calm my racing mind, I closed my eyes and slowly leaned my head backwards until it laid on his chest. I listen to the sound of his heartbeat and his breathing and after a minute my breathing ended up aligning with his and my head was no longer a storm. I slowly opened my eyes and met his own in the mirror getting lost in those icy blue eyes that have affected me since day one.

"Mind if I speak to Demon alone for a minute before the fight." I turn to see Xaiver and wondered how long he had been there, I hadn't even heard him come in here. Caiden Kissed the top of my head making me smile as he walked towards the door to leave. I walked over to the couch and sat down, Xaiver did the same.

"You sure this is a good idea? It's not to late to get you out of here." He asked making me chuckle.

"I have always admired your love for me X, you have been the father I not only always dreamed of having but the father that I desperately needed. I would be dead if it wasn't for you and I appreciate everything you have done to keep me safe, everything you have sacrificed. My parent's are smiling down at us and I know they are truly grateful for everything you have done, I Love you X but I need to get this over with even if it brings Marcus straight to me...It's time." I say as tears stream down both of our faces. He embraces me in a hug and I return it Graciously.

"I love you too." He mumbled trying not to cry, the door opened ending our moment and we turn to see tyler with a Fierce expression on his face.

"It's time." He said earning a nod from both Xaiver and I. We stand and follow Tyler down the hall towards the curtain.

"Caiden and Mike are next to the mat, Xaiver will join them, if anything goes wrong they will try to get on the mat to help but if they end up getting stopped like the fight with the twins then Jackson will be hiding in the crowd ready to move in like he did last time so they won't see him coming." I nodded as we waited at the curtain and Xaiver went ahead to announce the fighters.

It felt as if we were waiting behind that curtain for an eternity as we listened to Xaiver announcing raider and his brother then us. We walked to the mat with the crowd screaming our names but neither of us paid any attention to the crowd as our eye's were locked on our competitors. Raider stood next to his brother with a smirk on his face as he locks his eye's on me while Brad has a disgusted sneer stuck to his face though im not sure if it is because of how the crowd reacted to us v.s them or if it is because of Tyler but either way he isn't pleased.

We climb onto the mat after circling it once, locking our hands together and pressing our foreheads together we take a deep breath before turning to face Xaiver. X gave us a nod meaning good luck before returning his attention to the crowd.

"REMEMBER THIS IS THE UNDERGROUND SO YOU EITHER TAP OUT OR BLACK OUT!
READY...STEADY...FFFIIIGGGHHHTTT!!!" Xaiver roared as he backed off of the mat, let the fun begin.

Learning my lesson from the twins I trust tyler to focus only on brad and do what we have been training to while my eyes are locked on a smiling Raider. He sends me a wink before pulling his fight's up to a defensive pose but he isn't guarding face as he usually does and focuses mostly on his abdomen and this is one of his tell's meaning he has no intention of making the first move. taking a step close I keep one arm guarding my abdomen and chest while the other guards both my chest and face, I reluctantly plan the first move and I figured the only way im going to come close to beating him is if I not only tire him out but I also need to get behind him. I try side-stepping to make my way around him but he makes sure to match every step I take and keep his eyes on me. I'm just about to give up when I thought appears, Tyler's opening trick in that fight with Jackson, without another thought I charged Raider and he tried to swing just like Jackson did with Tyler and as if replaying that very fight I drop to my knees with enough force to slide me under raiders arm and as soon as I got behind him I stretch my leg out and spin my body knocking his feet out from under him and he is flat on the ground. Within second's I was on top of Raider throwing as many hits to his face as I could before the shock wore off and he brought his hand up to guard his face making me switch to throwing fast, hard jabs to his abdomen. After a few more blows to his chest I feel his abdomen tighten as he wraps his legs around my neck and slams my body to the ground knocking the air out of my lungs.

As I try and force air into my lungs Raider takes this opportunity to climb on top of he and get some painful blows to my stomach before switching to my face, the first hit connected with my lower lip busting it and the next two landed back to back on the right side of my cheek. Finally catching my breath I notice he isn't doing much in guarding his own body while he focuses on hitting mine, he never could focus on more then one thing at a time. I smirked before throwing two fast jabs to his abdomen making him grab it and bend over and when he did I sat up fast delivering a decent headbutt to his nose knocking him off of me. I quickly jump up and don't waste anytime, I need him tired in order to win this, im once again on top of him throwing blow after blow to both his face and abdomen but only able to get three hit's to his face before he blocked it so I focused on his chest and abdomen but am surprised by a harsh hit to my nose making blood pour down my face and I fell onto my back. My vision is clear but all the crowds cheering and screaming is quieted by the throbbing pain in my body, I look to my left trying to shake my senses back into my and see a bloody tyler delivering beast like hit's to an almost unconscious Brad. Time to finish this â€¦ I force myself onto my feet and put my hands up in a defensive stance as my eyes lock on a tired Raider doing the same. He had plenty of time to attack again and probably would have knocked me out but he used this time to try and catch his breath but he messed up because he let his body relax, now every hit will feel twice as hard. I walk towards Raider and when im a foot away I swing my body around and follow through with a steady kick to his face making his whole body twist as he slowly falls to the ground, unconscious I look over Tyler who was breathing heavy next to a bloody unconscious brad I give him a big smile before meeting him in the center of the mat, locking hands and pressing our foreheads together.

"We did it." I whispered with a smile as we pulled apart and turned towards the screaming crowd giving them a nod and walking to locker room, We won.

"Well shit." was all I was able to say.

CHAPTER SISTEEN IT'S THE TRUTH

CAIDEN'S P.O.V.

That fight was seriously nerve racking and both Tyler and Jay barley won, each with their fair share of cuts and bruises. By the end of the fight both of them were breathing rapidly and covered in blood but they did it and now we don't have to worry about that asshole, hopefully jay seems pretty sure he isn't going to hold up his end of the deal and stay gone but it has been a couple weeks since the fight and Raider hasn't made a sound, hasn't even showed his face once since he got knocked out.

I was walking out to my car about to grab some food and head to Jay's when my phone rang, I answered it not bothering to see who it was.

"Hello?" I answered

"We have a problem, meet me at the last place we talked in ten minutes." I heard Jake's voice making me stop in my tracks.

"Give me one good reason why I should meet with your sorry ass." I spat into the phone and rolled my eyes as I climbed into my car.

"Because if you don't Jay's life will be in danger." Was all he stated before ending the call.

"Shit" I muttered under my breath before pulling out of the driveway and making a beeline to the beach. When I got there I noticed it was pretty empty and not many people here, I walked all the way down the shoreline to the spot where Jake and I talked last time but he wasn't there. I look to my left and don't see anybody and come up empty handed again when I looked to my right as well as behind me. I face the water with a scowl on my face

"Asshole isn't even here." I muttered as I watched the waves crash against the rocks.

"May be an asshole but I am here." I heard Jakes deep voice say from behind me, making me jump and spin around.

"How the hell do you do that and will you stop doing it!" I all but yelled at him while he just smirked at me.

"Maybe you just need to be more observant." Jake smirked earning a glare from me.

"what do you want Jake, I thought you were leaving town." I asked and instantly his smirk was gone.

" I did, I left town. I listened to everything you said to me and I walked away to spare her anymore pain." He stated his voice sounding a little horse like he was trying not to cry. He went silent and closed his eye's taking deep breath's and once again I found my self feeling bad for him.

"She's happy you know, at least she seems happy." I stated in a low tone making him open his eyes and look directly at me. He gave me a pained smile as a tear rolled down his cheek.

"Thank you." He stated and I gave him a nod.

"But that breaks my heart more then anything because that is all over with, Marcus knows where she is and no doubt he is coming." Jake stated making my heart pound and my body started shaking fear ripping through me.

"No..." Was all I could spit out.JAY'S P.O.V.

I was out in my front yard washing my car when I saw Caiden's car flying up the driveway, he slammed on the brakes and jumped out of his car. I noticed someone in the car with him but with the tenting on the windows I couldn't tell who.

"What's going on?" I asked taking note of the panic on his face as he run's up to me.

"Jay look I don't know if your gonna be pissed but I think im doing the right thing and I need you to listen before you react." He stated with his voice trembling and by the way he called me Jay and not angel made my stomach churn. I furrowed my eyebrows together confused by what was going on and slowly nodded my head.

"What's going on out here we heard tires screech?" Mike, tyler, and Jackson came running out of the house as Caiden turned back to the car and nodded to whoever was inside of it. The car door opened and I could not believe what I was seeing I was about to charge at him before Caiden's voice ran through me like ice water

"Please Angel, it's important." Caiden said making me pry my eyes off of my Traitorous Ass of a brother, but as I looked into those icy blue eyes I can see the plea for me to listen and I know I have no choice...those damn eyes.

" It better fucking be because if not she is gonna have to leave you dumbass, you brought him to her home." Mike all but yelled at me making me tense up a little but when I look at a very quiet Tyler and chill's run down my spine. He has a bone shaking glare that radiates hate and betrayal but what made it worse was he was looking directly at Caiden, fists clenched.

"You fucking prick!" I heard Jackson scream as he tried to lunge at Jake but mike grabbed onto him and I jumped in front of Jackson so his eyes are locked on me, I shook my head no.

"Wait" I told him and waited on him to nod before I turned back to face Caiden

"I promise, you know id never do something like this if I didn't know it was necessary." He said to ty, but as much as I wanted to I couldn't understand why he would do this.

"Speak fast." I glared at Jake as he stepped closer to us.

"Can we talk in private littlebird?" He asked with almost pleading eyes that made me sick, tyler took a couple steps forward until he was right in front of me blocking Jake from me.

"Over your dead body." Tyler glared at him

"This doesn't concern you little boy." jake glared at Ty and this time it was me who stood infront of Tyler protectively.

"He is my brother, they all are my family so it does concern them. Disrespect any of them again and nobody will stop me from beating you to death this time." I spat at Jake making him tense up.

"Marcus found you Jay, and he is coming." Jake said and I felt my heart bottom out,

"Why...Why are you telling me this?" I asked not sure what else to say. Jake sighed and rubbed a hand over his face.

"I betrayed you in the past, I thought that life was better then what Marcus Threatened would happen but I was wrong. I won't watch you go through that again, I won't listen to you scream at all hours of the night. I messed up as your brother but I wont let him get you again. im warning you so you have time to run Jay, get out of here and don't look back." Jake finished and there was an eerie silence between us all.

"No...im done running. it's time for me to fight back Jake and it is time for you to leave." I stated before turning to leave.

"Let me help you Jay, let me make up for it." He said making me stop in my tracks. My heart I clenching right now wanting to trust him.

"I can't trust you Jake, you need to leave and this time don't come back, don't contact Caiden...disappear or I will kill you." I stated coldly before walking inside with Tyler right behind me.

CAIDEN'S P.O.V.

It has been about a week since I brought Jake to speak with Jay and Though she seems not to be upset with me anymore, Tyler still won't speak to me. I know I did the right thing, I know she needed to hear it from Jake I just wish he understood the way she did. I sigh heavily as I run my fingers through my hair, Jay is currently talking to Xaiver while matt is with her and tyler is here...at her house...glaring at me.

"Just get on with it already dude." I tell Tyler as I stand up and walk towards him. he stands and walks to me until we are face to face and I know what's coming. I know he isn't wanting to talk. Just as expected tyler drew back and gave me one hard punch to my gut making me topple over in pain.

" You put her in danger again Caiden and ill do a lot worse the a little punch to the gut, do you here me?" Tyler said with venom lacing his everyword sending chills down my spine.

"I thought I was doing the right thing Ty" I mumble still trying to stand up straight.

"That's the thing you didn't think, you have been meeting up with the guy who was responsible for how broken Jay is and you didn't even care, worse then that you brought him to the one place on earth she felt safe." Tyler said and I sighed he was right.

"Your right, I wasn't thinking and im sorry I just panicked bro." I said and this time it was him who sighed. he helped me stand up straight and walked me to the couch, the dude could fucking throw a punch from hell.

CHAPTER SEVENTEEN I'M READY

JAY'S P.O.V.

I sat in the living room with Caiden in perfect silence letting my thoughts run wild. After the new's of Marcus finding me got to us, thank's to jake, i have not been by myself, literally everywhere i go someone is guarding me but that is just putting me on edge even more because if marcus is really on his way then they are in danger around me. i sighed and looked at Caiden sitting next to me,

"I think you should stop coming around me for a while Caiden, it isn't safe. i think you all need to make yourselves scarce and quick." i said looking away from his beautiful blue eyes.

"That isn't going to happen angel, your stuck with me...and them." He said pulling me into his chest.

"Caiden, i don't want to loose you guys." I said trying not to sound defeated.

"You won't, ill always be with you...i promise." He said putting his thumb under my chin and gently making me look up at him. i stared into those icy blue eyes and forgot all my fears for that moment, it was just Caiden and I and nothing else mattered. He leans closer to me and glanced at my lips and i did not pull away. within seconds his lip's were softly kissing mine and tingles erupted where our lips connected. I wrapped my hand's around his neck and continue our kiss as he pulls me closer to him, after a few more seconds we both pull away to catch our breath and put our foreheads together.

"Am i interrupting something? " I heard Jackson's voice and i felt the heat rush to my cheeks at being caught.

"No!" I yelled and at the same time Caiden yelled

"YES!" making me turn redder and Jackson smirk wider. i shoot a glare at Caiden who just winked at me.

"Uh huh, anyways are you sure we should trust Jake, i don't get what he get's out of helping you now." Jackson said taking a seat across from us.

"I think we should take any threat as a real one, so if there is a possibility that Marcus found me and is on the way then we need to be prepared...just in case." I answered clearing my throat as Caiden smirked at me.

" Jackson, you need to leave. please go be with your girl, be happy, stop fighting...i need you safe." I said hoping he will be easier to convince then Caiden, Tyler, and Mike.

"Yeah not going to happen, ill go get my girl when this is over." Jackson smirked at me and i sighed in defeat.

"Whatever i give up, you all have a death wish." I growled and stood up stomping up the stairs and to the gym.

CAIDEN'S P.O.V.

Jake hasn't made a sound since Jay made him leave and i guess that is a good thing but it still feel's off. Now that kiss we shared the other night definitely did NOT feel off, in fact it is the only thing that has felt that right in a minute. I smile as i walk into the back yard and see Jay's swimming laps in the pool, she is breath taking.

"your drooling" i heard Tyler say from behind me and i smirk not taking my eyes off her.

"shut up" i reply and he chuckles

"So is it the right time yet..." he asked and i sighed shrugging

"How am i suppose to know when the right time will be, every time things are going good something get's in the way." i say frustrated.

"maybe the right time is now bro, things are about to get messy and she needs to know how you feel, and so do you." Tyler said and i know he is right, if i don't do this and something happens then i will regret it for the rest of my life.

"Your right, ill talk to her tomorrow. I want to do it right." I said already trying to figure out the perfect way to tell her... I love her.

An idea form's but i'm still not sure if it's good enough

"Hey what are you two up to." Jay asks pulling me form my train of thought and all attention on her as she wraps a towel around her damp body...fuucckk.

"Just trying to see if you would want to join me tomorrow for a couple hours. I have something i want to talk to you about?" I said smiling down at her as she looked at me curiously with those fire filled eyes.

"yea that sound's good to me, i could use a break from training." She chuckled and my heartrate sped up thinking that tomorrow i'll finally either get my girl or get my heart broken...hopefully its the latter.

"But for right now i need to go get dressed and go talk to Xaiver, ill catch you guys tonight." She said smiling up at me

"Later Angel" I smirked as i watched her walk off

"Damn what a view" I whispered to myself but forgot Tyler was right next to me and he smacked me upside the head

"HEY!" i yelled rubbing the back on my head

"You deserved it." He smirked before turning to walk away...maybe i did but i'd watch her anytime even if it end's up with me getting smacked by tyler.

JAY'S P.O.V.

I drove to the gym and parked my car next to X's. I walked into the gym and didn't see X in the main area so i headed to his office. the door was shut which usually means he want's to be left alone so i did the respectful thing a walked in not bothering to know. Xaiver was sitting behind his desk with a glass of whiskey in his hand.

"He you got a minute?" I asked closing the door behind me and taking the seat across from him.

"Depends, have you come to your senses and decided to get out while you still can?" He asked sarcastically knowing the answer but wanting to make it clear that he doesn't agree.

"Xaiver.." I sighed shaking my head no. he took a gulp from his glass before sitting it on the desk.

"What do you need?" He asked looking at me

"I need you to keep Tyler as busy as possible for me. If there is a fight he can take then give it to him, i talked to Raider and he is going to keep him busy for his own safety as well. i spoke with Stacy and she will keep Mike busy, now my only issue is Jackson and Caiden...they wont budge." I said running my fingers through my hair.

"I'll do the best i can, but for how long? Do we even know when Marcus is planning to show up?" Xaiver asked

"Not completely sure but Jake said he was on the way and i know Marcus won't waist time. He's coming...i can feel it. Just keep him busy until this is over with please." I all but pleaded with him and his gaze finally softened, he nodded.

"one more thing, if thing's go wrong when Marcus shows up...i need you to take care of them. Mike and Tyler have no home and family....if i get taken or die then the house is theirs. Try to look out for Caiden to the best of your ability." i said and smiled when he nodded in agreement.

"Thank you X, you will never know how much i appreciate everything you have done for me." I said as i walked around the desk and gave him a tight hug in which he returns it with his very own.

"I'm going to get going it's getting late and im pretty tired." I said pulling away from the hug and walking to the door.

"Call me if you need me." He said picking up his glass and drinking some more.

"If your sober enough to answer." I smirked before opening the door, he just smiled in return and shrugged. I walked out of the gym and to my car ready to be home. On the way home i thought of what Caiden would want to talk about and my heart flutters at the possibilities. Only one way to find out...

CHAPTER EIGHTEEN NO MORE RUNNING

CAIDEN'S P.O.V.

I ended up deciding to do a simple picnic. I got a red and blanket and a box of extra cheesy pizza, some sodas, and some daisies. Tyler help me set everything up by the river a mile from her house, i found it one day while taking a walk.

I walked inside her house and stopped when i saw her in the living room reading. she was wearing a pair of denim shorts and a white tank top with some cleats and a baseball cap, fucking hot.

"Damn..." I whispered catching her attention and she smiled shaking her head at me.

"You ready?" I asked trying to make my brain focus.

"Yea i'll just grab my key's, we can take my car." She smiled standing from the couch.

"No need, i figured we could just take a walk, there is something i want you to see." I smiled at her and opened the door for her to walk through. she smiled and walked out the door and i closed it behind me. We walked in peaceful silence half the way before she started getting anxious.

"Are we almost there?" She asked sighing.

"Almost just a little further." I chuckled as she sighed once again.

"So what did you want to talk about?" She asked as she looked at all the tree's and flowers.

"Well, to be honest i wanted to talk about us. Jay things have been hectic since the day we met and that isn't going away anytime soon but i can't keep waiting for the right moment when it may never come." i started and i could feel my heart start to race the closer we got to the river.

"Jay you have been my every thought since the day i stared into those fire filled eyes. All i want is to be close to you and it is getting harder for me to keep myself from holding you non-stop." I said stopping as we Came into View of the river and picnic i set up. it was a beautiful scene with a mini water fall and cherry blossom trees all around

"I love you Jay and i don't want to waist anymore time not being with you." I said turning to look her in her eyes and i saw the tears building up in them.

"I..." She started but was cut off.

"Well look who we have here." A deep gravelly voice came out of nowhere and all color left jay's body. i step to her left and turn around to see a big scruffy looking guy who sent chills down my spine standing a few feet away with raider right behind him.

"Marcus..." Jay whispered with her eyes locked on this man. shit...

JAY'S P.O.V.

I couldn't breathe, i couldn't move, i couldn't speak. All i could do was stare at my worst nightmare coming true, thankfully minus the gun...and Jake. i took a deep breath before glancing at Raider.

"So your the reason he found me." I said letting betrayal lace my forced, he looked at the ground refusing to meet my eyes.

"I did what i had to in order to get you back, he said we can be together when he takes you back." Raider said still not looking me in the eyes. i turned my attention back on the bigger threat.

"You know for year's i have been terrified of you, i have spent my life living in fear. Obeying, running, and hiding, always scared of you finding me...beating me. You took my entire soul from me Marcus, you stole my hope and joy and happiness but i no longer accept the hold you use to have on me." i said taking a step forward, confidence rising.

"This is my home... i found my hope, joy, and happiness here. i found who i was meant to be and i found my family and i will not return to any other life other then the one i have built." I said standing tall and proud.

"You act like you have a choice girl, ill drag you back or you will die where you stand." he spat reaching behind his back and bringing around a hand gun. Raider's eyes got wide and Marcus just smirked.

"You said you wouldn't hurt her." Raider said panic lacing his voice

"I wont kill her...unless i have to, now shut up!" Marcus yelled and my heart sinks...this is just like my dream but im actually thankful because if it wasn't for my dream then i wouldn't know how to end this.

"You may as well shoot me, i'll die before i return to that hellhole." I spat shooting a glare at marcus. He thought hard for a second before smiling

"Oh i figured as much...but will you let him die?" He smirked aiming the gun to my left and i looked at Caiden, know what is coming and knowing what to do to save him. I heard the hammer of the gun click back and quickly spun around stepping to the left and facing Caiden just as a gunshot rang through the fields.

"Nooo!!" I heard both Raider and Caiden scream. i felt a fire burning from my chest and look down to see red almost fully covering my white tank top. i looked up into Caiden's eyes as he grabbed me and i smiled at his beautiful eyes.

"JAYYY!!" i heard a mix of Jackson, Mike, and Tyler screaming my name and i assume they heard the gun shot and came running this way.

"Where...where â€¦ is ...marcus?" I said in between labored breathing looking into Caidens eyes

"Shhh he took off it's ok, your gonna be ok. Just stay with me." He said through sobs.

"Caiden..." I said and he snapped his eyes to my own waiting for me to speak

"I Love you.." Was all i said as Darkness surrounded me and all of their voices were tunneled out. everything was silent... and black, soon the pain left me too.

THE END?

Made in the USA
Columbia, SC
01 September 2023